James Crow

Cover design by Letitia Hasser of RBA Designs
http://designs.romanticbookaffairs.com/
All enquiries to JAMES.CROWAUTHOR@OUTLOOK.COM

First published 2016

for Roz

Chapter One

Do you dare?

Emma

I tapped Tommy's chest with the business end of the riding crop. 'Do *you*,' I said as he sat back onto a hay bale with a grin on his pretty young face, 'fancy a ride?' I trailed the crop down his shirt to his groin and prodded it. He was keen. I could feel it. The inexperienced always are keen. This is Tommy's first day as a stable boy. He's only nineteen. Ten years my younger. Keen and green, just how I like them.

He looked me up and down, stared at my tits; his mouth hanging open.

'I'll take that as a yes.'

I hooked him up with Jay, a trustworthy and gentle old steed, and myself with Gem a stunning chestnut redcoat.

We trotted off the yard and onto the track that opened onto the moor. I was already tingling with anticipation. Once out of sight of the stables and prying eyes I drew Gem to Jay's side. Tommy returned my smile. He went to say something but stopped when I pulled down the elasticated front of my summer top. The sun's warmth on my tits along with Tommy's gaping stare made my nipples tighten. Tommy licked his lips. I couldn't help but giggle.

A click of my tongue, a twitch of the reins, and Gem obliged with a canter. I glanced behind. Tommy was coaxing old Jay into action. It was half a mile to the first sheep pen. I gave Tommy a good look at my tits before hitting the gallop, my mind whirling once again with thoughts of cock. Any cock. I was determined to get my share before my life was ruined forever.

'Good girl, Gem,' I said as she slowed to a well-practised stop before the pen. Gem knew what came next. I hurried inside as Jay approached with Tommy on his back. The stonewall came up past my waist. I pushed down my jodhpurs and leant my elbows on the wall, my tits still on display. Jay came to a stop next to Gem. Tommy dismounted with an athletic flourish, boots thumping into the lush grass. His hands were at his belt buckle before he even entered the pen.

I stuck my arse out for him. Scratchy fingers probed and pulled at my wetness. 'Fuck me, Tommy. Quick! Fuck me!'

And he did. Rough and awkward and rushed and panting. And I loved it. He pulled at my breasts as he slammed against my arse and I know he came quickly but bless his heart he kept on going. I pressed my hands against the stonewall and met his thrusts and matched his grunts until the boiling spin in my belly ripped through my pussy and I yelled it out.

Tommy fell back to the grass, sweating, panting.

I thought it was my mother waiting at the gate as we returned to the stables and my heart almost stopped, but it wasn't my mother it was her sister, Aunt Fee.

Aunt Fee's an old hippie, all smock and beads and tousled hair. She lifted her glasses onto her nose as I dismounted.

'Darling,' she said, giving Tommy's arse a glance as he led the horses away, 'your fiancé and your dear mother need you in the drawing room. Pronto, I'm afraid.'

'What is it this time, how many gallons of rose petals to order for the confetti?'

She laughed. 'Don't be mean, Emma Jane. It doesn't suit you. Actually they want closure on the balloons.'

'Balloons?'

'Come,' she offered an arm. I linked it and we headed towards the house. 'Balloons for the church displays. Final colours and styles, you know the thing.'

'I don't really care, to be honest.'

'I know, dear. But let's get it over with quickly. There's something I need to talk to you about.'

'Oh?' We started up the steps to the rear courtyard.

'Hmm.'

'Tell me.' I figured I was going to get a lecture. *Do you really have to fuck all the stable boys, Emma Jane? You're getting married in two weeks, Emma Jane. Think about your betrothed, Emma Jane.* Blah, blah, blah.

'It's a surprise,' she said. 'Just wait and see.'

My betrothed, William, was bent over the oval table, Mother tight at his side, their heads stuck into balloon brochures.

They both looked up. William – a prize prick, sole heir to *Ripley's Gum & Candy*. He had his jacket off, sleeves rolled up, paunch pushing at his shirt buttons, the glisten of sweat on his brow as if this was hard work, which for him probably was.

'Ah, my princess,' he beckoned me over. 'We're thinking red, green, and silver for the balloons. Your mother's idea. It matches the company logo, you see?'

Yes, Mother would. 'I'd prefer blue,' I said.

Mother frowned. The opposite of her sister, Mother was a nun by comparison. A prim and proper nun at that. 'Emma, dear. We must think of the press. They'll all be there on the day. And after all, Mr Ripley is generously spending a small fortune to ensure your happy day is just so. The least we can do is consider the commercial opportunities.'

Of course we must. Mother had her eye on the prize. Father too for that matter. He'd made it no secret that marrying her off to a Ripley was his life's dream. *The family fortune will double within a year. The overseas opportunities for Winters Systems are there for the taking. And you're lucky, William is a good looker with a personal bank manager. What more could you ask?*

I could ask for a husband with a dick, that's what. 'Okay, have whatever balloons you want. I don't really care.'

Mother straightened, raised a finger, opened her mouth to speak. But Aunt Fee cut her off.

'I've an idea,' she said, taking me by the arm. 'I understand how stressful it can be planning a wedding. So I've arranged a surprise for you, and your mother thinks it's a super idea, don't you Rosalind?'

Mother smiled. So did William.

'What idea?'

Aunt Fee tapped her nose. She looked at her watch. 'Sign off those balloons and anything else that needs signing off, then come see me in the library.'

A surprise? I was intrigued. Aunt Fee liked surprising me. She'd done so all my life. A new dolly here and there; a new TV when I was older; a new horse when I was older still. I believe she did it to help redress the balance with my overbearing parents. And I loved her for it.

I signed off the balloons, and the ribbons for the cars in the same colours, as well as the flowers for the church, the reception, and my own bouquet. Mother had the idea of spraying some of the flowers silver. How jolly clever was that? I could have slapped her smug face and punched William's haughty beak.

I couldn't wait to get out of there and get back to the stables. Marcus was working this afternoon. I'd take him out and fuck him. Perhaps to the copse on Shotley Hill. Hell, I might even take Tommy and ride them both at the same time; the more the merrier before my *big day*. But first, Aunt fee. I made my way to the library with a spring in my step.

She was in the far corner, sitting in one of the green leather Chesterfields, typing at the laptop on the table in front of her. She waved me into the Chesterfield opposite and I couldn't help notice that familiar glint in her eye. I also couldn't help notice the bottle of champagne and two flutes, already filled.

'How did it go? The signing off?' She handed me a glass and we clinked them together.

I shrugged. 'I signed them off.'

'Hmm. Such a shame.'

'What is?'

She sighed and looked forlorn. 'My bloody sister. She listens to your father, no matter what. All she sees is pound signs and financial longevity. Sometimes I think I was given two hearts, and she, none.'

'Agreed,' I said, wanting to shout and scream and object and pout like a baby, but I was past all that. Way past it. I'd be marrying William Ripley, *no matter what*. No matter about my feelings. Father had slapped me on the back like a deal sealed. His own daughter. I took a swig of champagne. I love champagne.

'Listen, I told you I had a surprise for you.' Aunt Fee looked around as if searching for spies, then she lowered her voice. 'I've been thinking, about you screwing your stable boys morning, noon, and night, and I understand why. Good lord, I'd be doing the exact same thing in your position. Sometimes, my dear girl, I've found myself wishing I could whisk you away and give you some respite. And from those thoughts sprung an idea, and from the idea a plan.'

Her face glowed, eyes bright. I liked Aunt fee a lot. She always made me feel comfortable – wanted. 'Go on,' I said, seeing she was waiting for encouragement.

She emptied her glass in one go, pushed it across the table, indicted for me to fill up. So I drank mine down and refilled our flutes. 'Tomorrow afternoon,' she said, 'as you know, I'm flying to Italy for six days. I have one or two bits of business to attend to, and I will also be collecting your wedding dress, yes?'

I nodded a yes. I knew that much.

'Well, what would you say if I said you could come with me, have some *you* time, collect the dress with me. Six days away from this madness. How does that sound?'

'Really?' I rarely ventured beyond the stables. A socialite I was not. But alone time with Aunt Fee away from all this madness? Yeah, I could do that.

'Yes, darling, *really*. Perhaps we can change the wedding dress to red, green, and silver, ay?'

She laughed and I laughed with her. 'What about Mother?'

'I've already cleared it with your mother and William. I even convinced them that you would happily agree to leave the signing off of anything else that needs signing off entirely in their hands.'

It was a no brainer. 'I'm in,' I said, then the dirty girl on my shoulder reminded me I had a dozen stable boys to fuck. Then again, maybe I'd find some big-cocked Italians?

'You agree? Just like that? I thought you might miss your . . . *horses*.' She looked at me pointedly.

'There is that,' I said. 'but seriously, six days away from it all, and with my favourite aunt. It's just what I need right now. Thank you.'

She reached over and squeezed my knee. 'Now for the real surprise.'

'There's more?'

She patted my knee and sat back in her chair. 'That depends. Drink your champagne!'

I drank my champagne, the warmth spreading through my chest. 'Depends on what?'

She considered this while gazing towards the laptop on the table between us. 'The trip to Italy,' she started, 'it's all on, flights arranged, hotel suite, everything.'

I could feel there was a *but* coming. 'But?'

'But what if I said that was all just a front, a cover-up?'

Now she really did have that wicked glint in her eye. I pulled my legs up onto the chair and got comfortable.

'What I'm about to divulge is top secret, Emma. And I'm deadly serious about that, yes?'

'Okay. Mum's the word,' I said and instantly regretted my choice of words.

'I'm about to offer you an alternative trip. Everyone will believe you are in Italy with me, but you won't be. You'll be somewhere else.'

My heartbeat had noticeably increased. 'I'm intrigued,' I said.

'And whether you accept my offer or not, you must never tell a soul, yes?'

'Of course, Aunt Fee. Pinkie promise, you know that.'

Our pinkies met and tugged and she took my hand. 'Emma Jane, may I ask you a personal question?' I nodded. 'Your husband-to-be. Is he any good in the sack?'

I laughed at that. She squeezed my hand and let go. 'I thought as much.'

'He likes to do it once a week, on a Friday night, after drinkies with the chaps. And in the dark. Always with the lights off.'

Aunt Fee pulled a face. 'Well then, what would you say to a ride on a nice experienced dick for a change?'

If I hadn't just swallowed my champagne I would have spat it out. I couldn't speak. Did she really just say that?

'A big meaty dick at that,' she went on and I gasped, 'attached to a gorgeous blue-eyed man of muscle, wit, and, my God, when you see his tattoos.' She clasped a hand to her chest and sighed. 'And he's all yours for six days. Paid for by your Aunt Fee, a private little wedding gift from me to thee.'

'Paid for?'

'Oh, yes. Let me explain. Jonathon Gold is his name, and being a Master is his game.'

'A master what?'

Aunt Fee rolled her eyes and leaned forward conspiringly. 'He has a mansion in beautiful grounds not thirty minutes' drive from here, and a staff of angels, both male and female, who join in the *fucking* fun. He has dungeons and punishment rooms and fun rooms and dirty rooms and above all, Emma Jane, he has a big dick and knows how to use it!' She sat back, looking both flushed and pleased with herself at the same time.

I couldn't believe what I was hearing. 'You want to send me to a whore?'

'He's anything but a whore, Emma. Jonathon has rich clients, makes their fantasies come true with undivided attention. He'll spank you, fuck you, eat you all up; trust me, darling, you will have the time of your life!'

'He'll spank me?' I laughed. 'I'm not into that stuff.'

'Stuff? Have you ever been spanked?'

Nanny spanked me. Every day. The memories came thudding back. Under the stairs. No one around. Just nanny and me and her hand on my arse. I felt my arse burning just at the thought. 'No, I've never been spanked.'

'Whipped? Paddled? Had your breasts tied until they purple?'

'God no.'

'Then you haven't lived.'

'You're forgetting; I'm getting married in two weeks. I can't be getting whipped and tied or whatever else. My *betrothed* would surely notice.'

'It's all right, I've told Jonathon there must be no marking.'

'You've *told* him?'

'Of course. I had to speak to the man, to prearrange, so that if you said *yes* we could jump straight in.'

'So, you're going to Italy to pick up my dress. William and my parents think I'm going with you, but instead, I go and live in a mansion for six days getting screwed by a millionaire stranger.'

'Basically, yes. But don't go underestimating Jonathon Gold.'

I raised my eyebrows. 'And what kind of a name is that? Is it his real name?'

She let out an exaggerated sigh. 'You will spend six days with a master of everything sexual. He will show you new ways, delight your senses, wake you up to reality and, above all that, he will empower you. Trust me on that. This is an offer you simply should not refuse.'

'And if I do refuse?'

She took a sip of champagne, licked her lips, looked at me studiously. 'If you refuse, you can enjoy a trip to Italy, with me, and when we return, you can carry on screwing inexperienced youngsters with spotty arses, except on Fridays when you'll need all your energy to satisfy your limp-dicked husband. And you will remain ignorant of how it feels to be empowered, to be on top of your own world. The Master that is Jonathon Gold will give you that with knobs on, Emma Jane.'

The fly old fox. 'Might I ask how you know this *master*?'

She cleared her throat. 'I knew that would come up. I'll be straight with you. I'm one of Jonathon's clients. I visit him once a month, for a day of heavenly release and uplifting empowerment. The man and his den of passion thrills me.'

'Wow! Are you serious? Auntie Fee visits . . .' I held my tongue.

She gave me a stern look. 'A whorehouse? It's anything but a whorehouse. It's a pleasure palace, and nothing less. Mr Gold runs a stunning ship. His angels serve both him and the client equally. And I predict, my sweet and innocent niece, that once you have experienced Jonathon Gold's hospitality, you will return time and again.'

She passed me a business card. GOLD ESCORT SERVICES it said, embossed in gold, of course.

'Of course he really does supply escorts on a legit level. You can hire an angel to accompany you to a do, or to wine and dine you. But the real business goes on behind closed doors, and Mr Gold knows how to make his clients happy.'

'So I just turn up and he screws me for six days?'

'Basically yes, when you put it like that. Does the idea appeal?'

Did it appeal? I drank more champagne, topped up our glasses. 'What's he like, this Mr Gold?'

'He's a charmer, for sure. I know you'll like him.'

'How old is he?'

She laughed. 'Younger than me and older than you.'

'How much older?'

'I don't know for certain. Maybe he's nearing forty?'

I'm nearing thirty. What's ten years between a big dick and a needy pussy? 'Is he a looker?'

'Gosh, yes. Tall, dark, handsome. Trust me, you won't be disappointed.'

'So I just turn up?'

She turned the laptop towards me. 'This is the email confirming your appointment. All you have to do is press Send.'

Jonathon,

Confirmation of appointment. Six days.

Emma Jane – 6 p.m. tomorrow.

Ciao, Fiona x

'Note the lack of surnames.' She tapped her nose. 'First names only. Client confidentiality.'

My heart was thumping, cheeks flushed from the champagne, Aunt Fee grinning at me. It all felt surreal. 'What if I don't like it when I get there?'

'I've thought of that, too.' She handed me another card. *The Crab & Lobster* hotel. 'I've booked you a lovely themed cabin in the grounds.

Six days. Paid in advance. Told them you might not arrive at all, or that you might come and go, but to keep the room serviced for you. If you don't like what Mr Gold has to offer, you can hole up there until I get back from Italy.'

'You've thought of everything.'

She pushed the laptop towards me and raised her glass. 'Do you dare?'

Chapter Two

Six of the best

Jonathon

Mallory is client number One. My first big fish. Mallory likes pain. When she first came to me it was to experience a weekend of heavy BDSM. She wanted it all; to be spanked, whipped, caned, tied, strangled, poked and probed until she screamed the safe word.

Right now, Mallory is suspended from the ceiling by chains to the wrists. Her legs are held open by a spreader bar, and a vertical fucking machine is buried in her, ready to be fired up. I've already lashed welts into her back; I've already caned her tied tits; I've already caned her pussy until she screamed; I've already caned her thighs until the welts broke blood. She's panting, she's sobbing, but true to her word she is yet to utter her safe word.

'You have done so well.' I stepped up to the fucking machine and ran my hand between her legs. Her thighs and buttocks clenched and her chains jangled as she tensed.

'Thank you . . . sir.'

'Are you ready?'

She drew a ragged breath. 'I – I think so, sir.'

I tapped the cane against the fucking machine's metal shaft and the vibrations rang up through her. She let out a pleasurable moan. '*I think*, isn't good enough, Mallory. Tell me you want it!'

'I want it, sir. I want it.'

I pressed the switch on the fucking machine and the attached dildo pushed slowly into her. She groaned and writhed onto it. 'Give me permission to hurt you, Mallory.'

She gasped. 'You have permission to hurt me, sir.'

'To take you past your limits!'

'To take me past my limits, sir.'

I clipped the tops of her welted thighs with a light tap of the cane. She shrieked, arched into her chains, but the slowly twisting dildo held her in place.

'You look beautiful, Mallory. So beautiful.'

'Thank you, sir.'

'Tell me your safe word, Mallory.'

'Honeybee, sir.'

'Tell me I have permission to ignore your safe word.'

'You have permission, sir.'

'Good girl. Before we commence and take your senses to another level, tell me how many you want past your safe word.'

'Six, sir – six of the best.'

And that was the deal. Mallory was a retired headmistress. She knew discipline well, believed she could teach *it* a thing or two. Up until this point her buttocks had been left alone. While her breasts ached, while the welts on her back and thighs throbbed for mercy, those buttocks were clear, untouched.

I turned the dial on the fucking machine and the dildo squelched into her. She groaned again and pulled on her shackles. 'Oh, God, sir, please give it to me.'

I stepped to one side, where I knew she would be able to see my nakedness and my stance as I brought the cane back. It came down on her ass with a swish and a thwack. She screamed and shook and the dildo fucked her.

Thwack! She buckled and cried out for more.

Thwack!

'More, sir! More! More!'

An upward stroke, *Thwack!* And another. And she cried and begged for more as her juices ran down the shaft of the fucking machine.

I turned up the dial and stepped back once again. They would come faster now, that was the deal.

Thwack! Hard. The kiss of cane and flesh, straight centre, a red line across her ass. She roared the pain out, thrashed against the chains, and the fucking machine wobbled.

Thwack! Thwack! Thwack! Three, sharp and fast, straight centre again. Mallory bellowed her joy.

Ironic, to be delivering six of the best while I'm waiting for news of a possible new client.

Client number Six.

Thwack!

She intrigues me.

Thwack! Thwack! Thwack!

Six days of exploration and adventure with a novice.

Thwack!

Six days. No holds barred, so her friend says.

Thwack! Thwack! Thwack!

Mallory panted; her legs were shaking.

Thwack! A hard downward stroke, across the growing welts.

Mallory screamed.

We were close.

Six days. *Emma Jane.* I wondered what she'd look like.

Thwack!

I wondered if she'd last two days, never mind six.

Thwack! And again. *Thwack!* I caned Mallory's ass with rapid strokes. I counted at least a dozen before she screamed out her safe word.

I turned the fucking machine's dial to *Max* and stood back, allowed her to feel the rhythm, the heat, the inevitable burn of the growing orgasm. I would await her instruction, then I'd hit her, six of the best.

I noticed Angel Annabelle waiting at the door. The email I'd been waiting for? She was smiling. It must be good news.

'Now, sir.' Mallory groaned. 'I'm coming, sir. Do it!'

So I did it.

One, *Thwack!*

Mallory screamed blue murder.

Two, *thwack!*

I wondered if Emma Jane was a dirty girl.

Three, *Thwack!*

I wondered if Emma Jane had any kinks.

Four, *Thwack!*

Mallory was mewling and heehawing and bucking at the trembling dildo that was shafting her.

Five, Thwack!

Mallory's beautiful scream keened at my ears and I wondered if Emma Jane would scream with such pleasure.

And the *Sixth* – six of the best – I imagined Client Six hanging from the shackles, Emma Jane, her ass a lot younger, a lot peachier, an ass never touched before. I gave it my all for number six, ***Thwack!***

Mallory hiccupped, coughed, gagged, flapped like a hooked fish and trembled through an orgasm that I could almost feel myself. She'd reached that point, that half-light blur when pain becomes absolute pleasure; where pain takes on a life of its own.

I removed the fucking machine before unclipping the pulley and lowering her to the floor. Angel Harry was on hand to remove her restraints and see her through recovery in the adjacent treatment room.

I shrugged my robe on. With one arm around Harry's shoulder, Mallory took my hand and kissed it. 'Thank you, Jonathon, that was perfection. Your best yet.'

I took her hand and returned the kiss. She had my admiration; a woman empowered. 'Until next time,' I said and Harry helped her away.

Annabelle was at my side in an instant. 'Emma Jane has confirmed, sir. She'll arrive tomorrow, at six.'

My cock twitched at the very thought. Call it sixth sense, if you like. I had a feeling client number *Six* was going to be a game changer.

Chapter Three

Just go with the flow

Emma

'Still feeling sick?' asked Aunt Fee as the narrow country road took yet another rising curve.

Feeling sick? The butterflies in my stomach were doing the tango. I groaned as the road dipped and Aunt Fee took it too fast.

'Sorry, Emms. We're almost there.'

She pulled into a passing place and killed the engine. 'There it is,' she said and I followed her gaze through the windscreen. 'I park up here every time I visit Mr Gold. I get the jitters, too; the anticipation of it all.'

In the distance, perhaps half a mile, a huge redbrick mansion nestled amongst the greenery.

Aunt Fee took my hand, 'I'm jealous, truth be known. How about, when I pick you back up in six days, me and you spend a relaxing night at that Crab and Lobster hotel, and you can tell me all about your adventure? I'd like that.'

I squeezed her hand. 'I'd like that too.'

'Are you ready to meet Mr Gold?'

'As ready as I'll ever be.'

Six

We pulled up at the gated entrance at two minutes to six. The gates slid apart and the man in the gatehouse waved us through.

'How exciting,' Aunt Fee gave a little laugh.

I had to smile, even though I was absolutely crapping myself.

The driveway felt a mile long, curving through lawns and shady trees.

'You'll have a short interview when you arrive, not with Jonathon; with his PA. Just to agree the basics, sign non-disclosure, that kind of thing. Not your real signature, of course, just your first name to say you understand what you're signing up for.'

'Okay. Makes sense.'

'Oh, and Jonathon doesn't know we're related. Keep that to yourself. You're a friend in need receiving a special treat from yours truly, that's all.'

'Okay.'

'Then,' she cleared her throat, 'there's a quick medical before you're assigned . . .'

'A medical? You never said . . .'

'I didn't want to scare you off. Don't fret, Emma. They need to test you, make sure you're clean. Jonathon doesn't believe in condoms, you see.'

Good God! My heartrate was up again. 'Maybe you should have told me, Aunt Fee.'

'Look, we're here now. And there's Angel Annabelle waiting to greet you. She's sweet; you'll like Annabelle.'

Aunt Fee pulled the car onto the gravelled horseshoe. She flicked the switch for the boot and Angel Annabelle – a curvaceous blonde dressed in white polo shirt and white skirt above the knee – was already lifting my case out.

I took a long breath and blew it out. Aunt Fee touched my arm. 'Just do it, Emma. I promise you won't regret it.'

'I can leave at any time, right?'

'At any time. The Crab and Lobster do a delicious lamb shank.' She gave me her coy smile.

Angel Annabelle was waiting patiently outside, my case by her side. I took another deep breath, trying to calm the shakes that had started. 'Okay then. Wish me luck.'

'Good girl,' Aunt Fee said, 'and you, my favourite niece, don't need any luck. Just go with the flow, sweetheart, and you'll be glad you did.'

I kissed her cheek, we hugged, and then my sweaty palms were opening the car door.

Annabelle had a name tag on her breast pocket. She greeted me with a warm smile and a handshake. I followed her up steps, through double doors, and into a spacious foyer. Black and white marble tiles graced the floor, opening up to a wide staircase, white rails, red carpet on the stairs, paintings of naked couples in different sexual positions hung on every wall. The place was bright, airy, and smelled fresh and masculine.

I was shown into a small room just off the foyer. Annabelle left my case by the door and we sat at a desk that was bare apart from a printed form and a pen.

'Can I ask you a few personal questions, Emma? Is that okay?'

'Of course,' I said.

'Have you ever been tested for HIV?'

'No.'

She ticked a box on the form. 'Ever had a sexually transmitted disease?'

'No, never.'

'Good, good. Any blood disorders that you know of?'

I shook my head. 'Not that I know of.'

'Are you using contraception?'

'Yes, the pill.'

'Good, good,' she ticked another box.

'Have you ever suffered heart problems?'

'No.'

'Have any family members suffered heart problems?'

I had to think about that. 'I don't think so.'

'Have you had any broken bones or dislocations?'

Hell yes, where to start? 'Yes, I have. Multiple fractures to both arms, four broken fingers, a persistent thumb dislocation, and I've dislocated my right shoulder twice.'

She looked up from the form, eyebrows raised.

'Horses.'

'Ah!'

I repeated my calamities and she noted them down.

'Do you suffer from joint trouble at all?'

Did I? I was always aching after a hack. 'I don't think so.'

'Asthma?'

'No.'

'Any allergies?'

'Only hay fever.'

'No food allergies?'

'No.'

'Are you currently taking any medication?'

'Antihistamine tablets for the hay fever . . . and the pill.'

'Good, good.' She scribbled that down. 'Now, do you have any questions, any concerns?'

Did I? Yes. I had a whole list. *When would I meet Mr Gold? What would he do to me? Would he hurt me? Do I have to do everything he says?* My fingers were fidgeting, I was anxious, heart hammering.

'Emma?'

'Sorry . . . I'm . . .'

'It's okay, Emma. The first time can be a little daunting. It's natural to feel the nerves. But once we get you settled in, you'll be fine, so please don't worry.'

'Okay,' I said, and felt like the new girl at school. 'When will I meet Mr Gold?'

'That won't be until tomorrow morning. We'll get you settled in first.'

I felt myself relax a little, relieved that I wasn't going to be thrown into the deep end.

'Have you ever played the part of the submissive?' Annabelle looked straight at me, smiling pleasantly.

'No. I've never tried anything like that.'

'Oh, that's great.'

'It is?'

'Yes. Mr Gold is going to love meeting you, Emma.'

I could only smile. I felt like a wuss.

'I guarantee it. Don't worry, Emma. This is *your* experience. Nothing is going to happen that you don't want to happen.'

'What if . . . what if something goes wrong with, you know . . .'

'I understand your concerns, Emma, but trust that nothing can go wrong. You and Mr Gold will agree on a safe word, and you can use that safe word at any time to stop the experience.'

'And whatever's happening will just stop?'

'Absolutely. Your wellbeing and satisfaction are the only priorities. If you say *Stop* – it stops, and your care takes its place. Mr Gold knows what he's doing. And he does it well. We've never once had a dissatisfied client.'

I wondered what Aunt Fee's safe word might be. Sweet Jesus, I visit the same gigolo as my much older aunt, and we have safe words in case our asses are whooped too hard. I must be fucking crazy.

'And remember,' Annabelle continued, 'this is *your* experience. You may well be adopting the role of the submissive, but that is all it is – a role for you to enjoy. It is you who are really in control the whole time.'

Good point. It's just a role. What she said was true. I was in control. I was the boss here – at least of myself. *Just go with the flow, sweetheart*. 'Okay,' I said. 'Thank you.'

'You're welcome.' She marked an X at the bottom of the form, spun it around and slid it across the desk along with the pen. 'Before you sign the non-disclosure declaration and acceptance of our terms, let me tell you what happens next.'

I listened intently as Angel Annabelle told me that first I would have a quick medical with Nurse Barnett in the adjoining room. Nurse Barnett is sweet and will put me at ease. It won't take long. Then an angel will be assigned to me, a guide and mentor on call twenty-four hours a day. I will be shown to my room, where my mentor will prepare me to meet Mr Gold. Was I okay with that?

So I went with the flow, told her that was great, and signed *E.J.* in the little box. Nurse Barnett was really sweet, and quick. She weighed me, checked my blood pressure, swabbed me, took blood from me. When I returned to Annabelle she was chatting to another angel, a small girl, dressed in the same white polo shirt and skirt. She broke away from Annabelle and came towards me with an outstretched hand.

Suki was the name on her breast pocket. This girl was smaller than me, if that was even possible. A black bob of hair and a smile so wide it almost hid her eyes. I guessed she was Japanese; she reminded me of a friend from my schooldays. 'Hello, Miss Emma, my name is Suki. I am your mentor for your stay.'

For a small girl she had a firm handshake. I returned the smile. I liked Suki from the off.

Annabelle thanked me, said she would see me again soon, and Suki led me away, pulling my suitcase along behind her.

My room was on the first floor, just off the landing. Room 6.

It was much bigger than I'd expected. The main living area held two king-size beds, a two-seater leather sofa and chair, a chaise longue, dresser, minibar, tea-making facilities. There was a walk-in wardrobe and once again everything was bright and airy. The en suite was just as big. To one side a Jacuzzi big enough for four; to the other side an open shower with multiple jets; a huge mirror above the sink in the shape of wings – angel wings, I realised. All of this was backlit by soft blue lighting.

'It's a beautiful room,' I said to Suki who had boiled the kettle and was now making tea.

'They lovely rooms, Miss Emma. All angels have same room as guests.'

'You live here? Full-time?'

She handed me a steaming cup and I joined her on the bed. 'All angels live here. We big happy family.'

She certainly appeared to be happy. She only looked about twenty. I wondered what her story was.

'You like the tea?' she asked.

I took a drink. It tasted a little spicy, but it was refreshing. 'I like it very much.'

'From Japan, special aph-ro-dis-i-ac,' she spelled the word out, 'make you horny for Mr Gold,' then grinned from ear to ear.

I wasn't sure if she was joking or not but couldn't help smiling back. I was starting to relax, and realising that Suki would be by my side made the whole thing seem less daunting.

My phone beeped in my suitcase. I retrieved it from the zipped pocket. A text from Aunt Fee.

Are you going with the flow? Love you xx

I text back:

The flow's good. I'm going with it. Love you too xx

'Oh, Miss Emma,' Suki was looking at my hand, at my engagement ring. 'Can you remove rings for your stay please? No rings allowed in case of accident.'

My engagement ring, a single diamond. It really was beautiful. If only the man I was being forced to marry wasn't such a self-centred prick. I took it off gladly and enjoyed a sense of release as I placed it on the dresser.

Suki showed me the menu for room service, whatever I wanted, day or night, just hit 6 on the phone and my wish is an angel's command.

'I recommend the six seasons pizza, Miss Emma.'

'*Six* seasons?'

She nodded eagerly. Her black bob shook about her head. 'Mr Gold invent special pizza for special client.'

'Oh?'

'You, Miss Emma, special client number six.'

And I was in room *six*. And to dial out on the phone I had to press *six*. A nice touch. But only six clients? I queried that with Suki.

'No, no, Miss Emma. Mr Gold has great many clients. Only special ones get numbers.'

'And I'm special because?'

'Because many things. Because you long stay. Because you new to sex.'

'New to sex?' I laughed at that. 'Hardly.'

'Submissive is new for you. Sub sex like no other sex. Specially with Mr Gold.'

'What's he like, this Mr Gold?'

Suki giggled, her pale complexion flushed a little and she hugged herself. 'Mr Gold is lovely man. When he hold you, he hold you just right.' I noticed her eyes had glazed over. She clearly adored him. 'And he touch in all right places, Miss Emma. He so good with his hands.'

'What does he look like?' Aunt Fee said he was tall dark and handsome but I wanted more than that.

'Oh, Miss Emma. Sorry, but I'm not allowed to say.'

'Please, Suki, give me something. Anything.'

'Okay,' she said with a grin. 'I tell you one thing.'

I was all ears. 'Go on.'

'He has beautiful eyes,' she'd lowered her voice to a whisper. 'Blue like the sea. Kind eyes. And when he smiles, my heart always melt a little. He gorgeous, Miss Emma. A good man. But please don't tell anyone I told you.'

'I won't tell. He does sound nice.'

Suki nodded. 'You will love him, Miss Emma. Are you excited to meet him?'

'A little nervous,' I admitted. Although it wasn't for meeting him, I realised; it was for fucking him, or him fucking me. It's a big leap from screwing inexperienced stable boys to getting it on with a guy who does it for a living. What if I was a failure? What if I didn't satisfy him? Was I even meant to satisfy him?

Suki took my hand. 'Of course you nervous. But Suki here. You be fine.'

Jonathon

I pressed Rewind for the umpteenth time, this time all the way back to when the car comes into view, and I watched, frame by frame. Sunlight made the car's interior dark. Only shadows, all the way. The car pulls up, Annabelle steps into view. The two figures in the car – Fiona and her friend – are talking, saying goodbye. The shadows move together, a kiss on the cheek. The door opens and she steps out.

I pressed Pause. She's small, petite, with a good curve to the hip, a pinched-in waist. She would look good in a corset. She's wearing a cream blouse and a knee-length tartan skirt with pleats. Her footwear, practical black pumps.

I brought the magnifying icon to her face and zoomed in. The picture was fuzzy, no real detail, but she looked nice, a symmetrical beauty, with auburn hair just off the shoulder. Fiona said her friend was a dirty girl, and I couldn't wait to find out.

Chapter Four

Anticipation is foreplay

DAY ONE

Emma

I was in an exotic dreamland, where the moors were aflame and Gem galloped like a warhorse, my breasts bouncing deliciously and my naked butt thumping into the saddle. The orgasm rang out in ripples like a pealing bell, the flames shimmering ahead of me, sweat splashing off my breasts, and the ringing intensified until I cried out . . . and I was awake, only the soft blue backlighting – and the ringing phone.

Six a.m.

'Hello?' I croaked into the handset. The voice that came back, deep and smooth, brought me wide awake.

'Good morning, Emma Jane. I'm Jonathon. Jonathon Gold. I trust you slept well?'

'Thank you. Yes. Yes, I did.'

'I'm glad to hear it. Suki will be with you shortly. I look forward to meeting you.'

Meeting me? Does he mean fucking me? He hung up. I put the phone down and stared at it, his words repeating over and over. *I look forward to meeting you.* Shit. This was it.

Six

The door opening made me start.

Suki walked in, bright and cheery. 'Hello, Miss Emma. You have good sleep?'

She sat on the bed and took my hand.

'Have I got *terrified* written all over my face?'

'Just a little bit,' she said and patted my hand. 'Suki make tea.'

I was glad of the tea. It did seem to take the edge off things. I drank the last of it and made to jump in the shower but Suki stopped me.

'No time for shower. We must go soon. Mr Gold waiting. Also, Mr Gold wants you to dress in same clothes you arrived in.'

I screwed my face up. 'Really? They'll be a bit stinky.' *I'll* be stinky!

Suki smiled her bright smile. 'Mr Gold like natural smell.'

I grabbed some fresh underwear from my suitcase but Suki caught my arm. She shook her head. 'Same underwear, too, Miss Emma.'

'How do you feel?' Suki asked as she held the room door open for me.

My legs were trembling, my heart fluttering, and I felt dirty in yesterday's clothes. A dirty girl being led to the headmaster. 'Butterflies are rocking the shit out of my tummy,' I said.

Suki rubbed my arm. 'Come on, you be okay.' She linked into me as we descended the staircase and I held on tight, my legs were shaking so much. Christ, and I was meant to obey this man? Let him touch me? I felt like a failure before this had even got started.

We ended up at a plain white door with no markings.

Suki took my hands. 'You ready?'

I took a breath. 'I think so,' I said, then, 'are you coming with me?'

'Suki wait outside, but you be okay.' She gave me her heart-melting smile and held a fist up to the door.

Words of objection whirred through my mind . . . *I've forgotten to take my hay fever tablet; I've forgotten to take my pill; I need the toilet, desperately.* Suki rapped on the door.

'Come,' said the familiar smooth voice from within.

And that was it. Suki was opening the door and pushing me through it.

The windows were shuttered and the room was dimly lit by three or four table lamps. A desk, filing cabinets, a small chair in front of the desk and beside it what looked like a therapist's couch in black leather. And on the wall a huge TV screen flanked by paintings of nudes in bondage.

The man himself was standing at a filing cabinet behind the desk, his back to me. Dark ruffled hair, grey suit. Taller than tall. Wide shoulders. He slid the cabinet drawer shut and turned. White open-necked shirt, tanned skin beneath. He just looked at me, standing by the door like an idiot.

'Hello. I'm Emma,' I said.

'Come to me,' he said, moving to his desk.

I arrived at his desk in a blink, wanted to sit, couldn't. Had to wait. For him to say, to speak. His face was partly in shadow but he was smiling. He told me to take a seat and we both sat at the same time, he into a high-backed chair that swivelled as he settled, me into a chair that was hard and uncomfortable.

'Jonathon,' he said, offering a hand over the desk. When I leaned in to take it I caught his eyes, sea-blue and beautiful, just like Suki had said. Strong features, prominent brow and a cheeky smile complete with dimples. It might have been the lamplight but there was a definite glint in his eye. Aunt Fee wasn't lying; this man was gorgeous.

His touch was firm but gentle. My hand felt like a delicate bird in his. He gave it a slight squeeze before letting go. 'How are you this morning?' he asked.

I swallowed away my dry mouth. 'I'm good. Thank you.'

'I'm pleased to hear it.' He looked at a sheet of paper on the desk, ran a finger down it. I recognised it as the form Annabelle filled in yesterday. 'I do have one concern, Emma.'

I clasped my hands in my lap.

'You've twice dislocated your right shoulder. When did the first dislocation occur?'

'About a year and a half ago.'

'How did it happen?'

'My horse, she was spooked by an owl, flew out of the grass right at her feet. She reared and danced sideways at the same time. When she took off, I was off balance, my boot caught in the stirrup, dragged for a hundred yards or so before she came to a stop. Broke my arm, added a broken finger to the broken-finger collection, and popped my right shoulder.'

'That must have hurt?'

Like a bastard. 'Yeah, it did.'

'And the second dislocation, when and how?'

I remembered it well; the screaming, the agony. 'About two months later. I was slinging a saddle over the top rail and it went. Just like that.'

'And lately, has it shown any signs that it might give?'

I touched my shoulder, shrugged. 'No, it feels fine.'

'Any aching from the joint?'

I realised I was beginning to relax, the tone of his voice so soothing. 'When there's a frost on the ground, I have to keep it wrapped up.' I also realised I was sounding like a moaning old woman. 'But I'm fine, really.'

'I'm sure you are. Have you ever been shackled, Emma Jane?'

His words took me by surprise and my stomach rolled as I imagined his hands clasped around my wrists. 'No,' I said weakly. *Breathe, Emma, breathe.*

'I like to hang my submissive, you see. But I'm concerned about your shoulder.'

Hang? 'Okay.'

'Should I be concerned, Emma?'

Should he? 'I don't know.'

He sat back in his chair. 'Let us be aware of it, then. Be cautious.' I nodded, visions of me swinging by one arm came to mind. Jesus! 'Which brings me to *marking.*'

He let the word float in the air between us. Goosebumps ran up my arms.

'Your friend stipulated that marking was not an option.'

'Yes,' I almost called him *sir*. I don't know why, 'that's right.'

He pulled a desk drawer, lifted out a notepad and pen and pushed them to the corner of the desk.

'Do you understand the role of the submissive, Emma Jane?'

Did I? 'Not entirely,' I almost called him *sir* again. What the hell was *that* all about?

'Ultimately, the submissive brings pleasure. She does this by giving herself, her body, her mind, her trust, and in doing so the pleasure of giving is felt by the submissive herself, resulting in a perpetual circle of bliss. Isn't that poetic?'

'Poetry in motion,' I said, and felt pleased with myself.

He gave an appreciative laugh and his eyes sparkled. 'Stand up,' he said.

I did, legs shaking. I smoothed my skirt down.

'Please relax,' he said, getting to his feet. He took off his jacket and hung it over the back of his chair. He turned his sleeves up, and came around to the front of the desk, where he rested his butt against it. He smelled like a pine forest in autumn. My stomach seemed to be rocking back and forth. I tried to stare straight through him but couldn't. I could only focus on his tanned chest, the muscle definition beneath his shirt.

'Anticipation, Emma Jane, is a wonderful thing. I could spank your ass pink right now, and believe me it's tempting. But I won't. I'll enjoy the wait, as will you, each in our own way. You are feeling two things; the first is fear . . . fear of me, a stranger, seeing and touching you intimately. And the second is also fear . . . fear of the pain. Am I right?'

My face was burning; my pussy was heating up. He was bang on. 'Yes.'

'As my submissive, the first thing you must learn is to alter that fear. Realise that anticipation is foreplay, and that pain is the purest form of pleasure. Foreplay and pleasure, Emma Jane. No fear. Never fear. Does that make sense?'

It did make sense. But that didn't mean I wasn't still crapping myself. 'Yes. I think so.'

'Good. Now, please make yourself comfortable.' He indicated to the therapist couch behind me.

I was glad to get off my feet. The couch was soft. I lay back, illuminated from the lamp on the table by my side. I felt like a specimen under the spotlight, which to him I probably was.

He picked up the notepad and pen and brought the small chair I'd been sitting on. He positioned it alongside, close, and sat with one leg crossed over the other, the notepad resting on his knee.

'You will call me *sir* from now on. Yes?'

'Yes, sir.' *That felt strangely better.*

'Good. I'd like to establish your likes and your dislikes, and your desires, of course. Tell me what you desire, Emma Jane?'

I felt myself relaxing, sinking into the soft leather couch. His words, his voice. He melted me.

'Take all the time you need, Emma.'

I looked at the man sitting so close, his broad upper body well-defined beneath his shirt, his strong hands. His eyes caught mine and I looked away. What did I desire? I was here for sex, wasn't I? Here to experience the best sex? 'I desire good sex, sir.' He let my words hang between us. I could feel his eyes on me. 'I . . . I haven't,' I swallowed away my dry mouth and plucked up the courage to look at him, at his sea blue eyes. 'I haven't been with anyone experienced, sir.'

He nodded, wrote on the pad. 'Then I promise you, Emma Jane, you will not be disappointed. You smell lovely, by the way.' He can smell me. *I* can smell me; yesterday's sweat. 'The natural scent of a woman is so much more alluring than any contrived perfume, I always find.' He smiled at this, a sparkle in his eyes. 'Hmm.' Looking straight at me. 'Are you a dirty girl, Emma?'

Oh, still my beating heart. Was I? Does fucking three stable boys a day make me a dirty girl? I certainly felt like a dirty girl right now, in yesterday's clothes, perspiring, hot between the legs for this cheeky Adonis. Because that's what he was. An Adonis. And he's going to fuck me. I bit the bullet. 'Yes, sir. I think so.'

'Have you ever ridden a man's face, Emma Jane?'

My pussy clenched at his words. I saw myself bucking on his head between my legs. Jesus! 'No, sir. I've never done that.'

Six

'Ever sucked on a woman's breasts?'

What? 'No, sir.'

'Had sex with a stranger?'

'No, sir.'

'Anal sex?'

I felt my ass clench. 'No, sir.'

'Anal insertions?'

Christ! 'No, sir.'

'Rimming?'

'What?'

'Tongued arse, Emma. Have you ever had a tongue up your arse?'

I swallowed. 'No, sir.'

'Then you have never tongued an arsehole?'

'No, sir.'

'Ever been whipped or caned?'

'No, sir.'

'Spanked?'

Only off Nanny. 'No, sir.'

'Are you certain?'

Does he know? 'Yes, sir.'

He smiled at me. 'Were you spanked as a child?'

I stared at my shoes.

'Who spanked you, Emma?'

'My nanny. Nanny Carter. She'd spank me.'

'How did it make you feel?'

'I was only little, but there was something about it. Something in the sting.'

'How old?'

'Maybe five or six.'

'Six,' he scribbled on his pad. 'And how did you deal with those feelings?'

My God. The memories.

'You can tell me, Emma. Tell me what you did about those feelings.'

'I touched myself, sir.'

'And?'

'I . . . my father's chair, when he was at work, it had bare wooden arms, all smooth and hard. I'd be in my nightdress. After Nanny spanked me, I'd straddle the arm of Father's chair, and ride it, like I was riding a horse.'

'And now you ride horses every day.'

'Yes, sir.'

'And this brought the younger you satisfaction?'

'Yes, sir.'

'Tell me what it felt like.'

I could feel it right now, the smooth arm of the chair, my weight pressing onto it, the rubbing back and forth. 'I remember the heat, intense heat, pulling through me. It always made me smile.'

'Good girl. Take yourself right back there, Emma. How long did this go on for?'

'Until the day Nanny caught me. It was so strong, the feeling, that I screamed and Nanny came in. She sat in Father's chair and put me over her knee and hit me until I was crying and begging her to stop.'

'And you refrained from riding the chair arm after that?'

I was right there, over Nanny's knee, the tears, the humiliation, and the feel of the hard chair arm between my legs. I could feel myself squirming and I was speaking before I realised, 'The rug . . . in front of the fireplace . . . I was watching TV, felt an itch. I rubbed the itch against the rug, and before I knew it the heat was pulling through me again.'

'So you started getting off on the carpets?'

When you put it like that. A nervous laugh escaped me. 'Yes, sir.'

He laughed too, and his smile made me smile. 'Your nanny didn't catch you?'

'No, sir. But I did get caught. I thought that if I took it slow, kept the movements short, I could do it while my mother was in the room and she wouldn't notice.'

'But she did notice?'

'Yes. One day the vicar was coming for tea. She took me to one side and explained that rubbing myself on the carpets was a rude thing to do, and that I should be discreet and keep rude things for the privacy of my bedroom.'

'She'd known all along what you were doing?'

'Yes, sir. I feel embarrassed just thinking about it.'

'Please don't feel embarrassed. Sometimes, little girls can be dirty. The need within makes itself known, makes the girl explore. And as the girl grows older she finds new ways to experience the pleasure between her legs.' His eyes again, so knowing. 'You are no longer a little girl, Emma. You can explore, find those new experiences and feel comfortable with it.'

Something in his tone, suggestive, naughty, as if he was the one that wanted to explore *me*, brought tingles to my pussy. I shifted, fidgeted.

'After that, did you keep your rudeness to your bedroom?'

'Yes. Yes, I did, sir.' *Please don't ask.*

Silence.

I caught his eye again. Smiling. Waiting.

'You found a new way?' he eventually said.

My face was burning up. *I* was burning up.

'What happens here is between you and me, Emma. You can tell me.'

I stopped wringing my hands, took a breath. 'I found . . . I used . . . it . . . it was my hairbrush, sir. I would brush myself. The bristles felt nice. I'd do this over and over . . . until I was sore. Then one day, I . . . I just pushed the handle inside. And that felt even nicer. The heat came quicker. It was a revelation.'

'I'm sure it was. Do you have a vibrator at home?'

'Yes, sir.' *I didn't want to tell him I had a dozen of the things.*

'Do you have any kinks, Emma Jane?'

'Kinks, sir?'

'Like clipping clothes pegs to your nipples, or dancing naked in the rain. What turns you on, Emma Jane?'

Christ, Mr Gold, you *turn me on.* 'In the saddle, sir. On the moors where no one can see me. I like to ride topless, gallop, the harder the better.'

'Interesting,' he said, then tapped his pen against the notepad.

I could almost hear him thinking. I just knew what he was going to ask.

'Have you ever been caught?'

'Yes, sir. And it was crazy. Really crazy. I came face to face with a rambler. An old guy.'

'I hope you didn't give him a heart attack.'

I heard myself giggle. He smiled at that. 'No, sir. I think he enjoyed it.'

'I'm sure he did. What did he do when he saw you?'

'Stood there with his mouth hanging open. He started playing with himself.'

'And you stayed there until he had finished, dirty girl?'

Another flourish of tingles danced through my pussy at his words. I could feel the wetness between my legs. 'Yes, sir. I stayed while he played.'

'Did you encourage him? Put on a show?'

Yes, of course I did. I was a dirty girl. 'I stood up in the stirrups, shoved my jodhpurs down and rubbed myself. He fell to his knees and came on the grass with a grin on his face. I rode off laughing . . . and came in the saddle on the way home.'

Mr Gold uncrossed his legs. He put the pad and pen on the desk. I noticed the fullness of his trousers, the tailored fit, the alpha male on show.

'You please me, Emma Jane. You are a dirty girl. Tell me what you think about while you're playing. What fantasies do you have?'

I noticed my heart was louder, my breathing too. 'Sometimes, when I'm . . . when I'm playing, I imagine driving down the motorway in an open-top car. I'm naked and the wind is blowing right through me and other drivers toot their horns as I pass.'

'Nice,' he said. 'Do they catch you and fuck you?'

'No. My next stop is a park. There's a sexy guy on a bench, eating his lunch, and I walk right up to him.'

'Still naked?'

'No, I'm dressed again. There's no one else around. I sit by his side and . . . I expose myself. And when he gets his cock out I take hold of it, and relieve him.'

'How?'

'With my mouth and my hands.'

'And when he comes, so do you and your fantasy is over?'

'Yes, sir.' I could feel the pulse in my clit, the need to touch it.

'What happens next, Emma Jane?'

I wanted to lie. I wanted to tell him that was it. But my silence betrayed me.

'Would I be right in saying that the fantasy gets dirtier? Maybe even outrageous?'

I took a breath; my cheeks were burning. 'Yes, sir.'

'Then tell me.'

'It's just a silly fantasy, sir. I would never do it for real.'

'I understand that. Please, tell me what is it that you orgasm to?'

My chest was rising and falling too fast. My nipples were hard. I could see them poking through my blouse. *Just go with the flow . . .* 'It's sex with a girl.'

'A girl that you know?'

'Not really. It could be a movie star. Or just a girl with no face.'

'What kind of sex do you engage in?'

'It's almost primal. Touching, feeling, stroking, hugging a naked woman close, kissing, licking, nibbling.' *Jesus, just touch me, Mr Gold.*

'What else?'

Could I really tell him this? 'Well . . . sometimes . . . sometimes it gets really wild.'

'Yes, go on.'

'I imagine . . . I imagine that our hands are fucking each other, then my head is between her legs and hers between mine. We . . . we eat each other like savages. And . . . and as I come, as *we* come . . . there's . . .'

He stared at me, waiting. And I was burning up.

'There's what? Tell me, Emma Jane.'

I looked to my knees, smoothed out my skirt. 'Well . . . there's . . .

there's pee. A lot of pee. I can't believe I've just told you that.' I was breathless. Burning up and breathless.

'What a beautiful fantasy. Well done, Emma.' His hand came down to rest on my knee and I flinched at his touch. Tingles sparked from my pussy to my breasts as he shifted from his chair and sat on the edge of the couch. His hands were on my knees, parting them. There was a glint in his eye, 'I am going to make you come now, Emma Jane.'

I gasped at his words, my legs trembling.

'Emma Jane. Look at me.' I stared into his beautiful eyes. My breaths were ragged. I didn't hide the fact. I went with it. He knew I wanted him. He took hold of my skirt and lifted it back, exposing my thighs. The warm touch of his hands as they slid slowly upwards sent tingles dancing through me. A trickle of wetness touched my inner thigh. I wanted him to find it, touch it, lap it up.

His hands moved to the sides of my thighs and he took hold of my panties and gave a little tug. I gasped as he pulled them away from me. He tugged them to my knees and raised my legs and in a heartbeat his fingers were at my pussy lips, stroking, parting them gently. I moaned into it, closed my eyes and savoured his gentle touch as he slid a finger up and down, my lips flowing around it.

On the upstroke he caught my clit, lightly, and my body leapt. He slid a finger into me and held it there. No. Two fingers, moving them against my inner walls. Moving them in and out, up and down, catching my clit again and again, and I moved with him, riding the sensual rhythm, his delicate touch. I couldn't stop, didn't want him to stop . . .

'You have a beautiful pussy,' he said, three fingers now, pushing deeper.

I let out a groan and heard myself asking for more.

'Have you ever shaved your pussy, Emma Jane?'

'No, never,' I gasped.

'Sir!'

'No, never, sir.'

'When smooth and clean, the sensations from a good fucking are taken to new heights.'

He worked me faster, twisting his fingers in and out, and I grabbed at my raised legs as my thighs rippled and my clit throbbed.

'Would you like me to fuck you with your pussy shaven, Emma Jane?'

'Yes, yes,' I said, breathless.

'Good girl. I'll have Suki see to that.'

Suki? Oh, God.

It happened so quickly. His fingers curled inside me while his thumb found my clit and he pressed them together and hit the fucking spot. I cried out and my pussy gripped him as he rocked me back and forth. My ass raised from the couch and I heard myself shrieking, the orgasm exploding through my clit in painful bursts of pleasure as his fingers pummelled me. I cried it out, 'Yes! Yes! Oh fucking yes!' shuddering violently as he wrenched his hand away.

Jonathon

I called Suki in and asked her to prepare our guest.

I watched them go, and smiled as Suki took hold of Emma's hand.

Emma Jane. The woman captivated me. This wasn't like the other times, worldly-wise women drenched in expensive perfume, demanding a punishing fuck; demanding great heights of ecstasy before they returned home to their clueless husbands. Emma Jane was different; inexperienced yet eager, dirty yet cautious, hesitant yet willing.

Six was a diamond among gems, a truth among lies.

Six was just perfect . . . and I was going to give her the fuck of her life.

Chapter Five

The Shave

Emma

I returned to my room in a daze. I could still feel him down there, his grip as he brought me off; his thumb catching my clit at just the right moment. It was heaven, an incredible climax. I sank onto the edge of the bed and relaxed into the high, savouring the unfamiliar soothing feeling of the come down. I wanted more.

Suki produced a bottle of champagne from the minibar and poured two glasses. 'To celebrate first come,' she said and we clinked glasses. 'You lucky, Miss Emma. Clients don't usually get to come so soon.'

'They don't?'

Suki shook her head and grinned. 'No, they don't. Drink up!'

I took a sip of champagne, enjoyed the fizz on my tongue, then downed the lot in one go, much to Suki's delight. She poured me another.

I was about to ask what happened next but didn't. I knew what happened next. I could hear his voice in my head, caught snippets as he talked to Suki. He was going to fuck me. And before that happened I would be shaved, by Suki. Christ this was all so surreal. I drank the champagne and held out my glass for more. I noticed Suki had only sipped at hers.

In my head she was touching me, shaving me smooth, fingers probing, and the girl in my fantasy would no longer be faceless, and . . .

'Miss Emma,' Suki was there, right in front of me. She handed me my refilled glass. 'You okay?'

'Yeah,' I said, but my pussy was burning, my heart racing.

'Maybe you nervous for shave?' She looked at me doe-eyed.

God she was pretty. A little doll. 'Yeah,' I took another drink of champagne. It was going down well. 'Can I shower now? I really need a shower.'

'Of course,' Suki said, 'then we do shave.'

'Do we have to? I'm not sure, you know . . . I mean, I could do it myself, in the shower.' But my words were weak.

Suki stepped back from the bed, shaking her head. 'No, Miss Emma, shave must be excellence.' She lifted her skirt. Thin white legs with a gap at the top, and the smoothest cup of pussy with a hint of pink slit. 'Suki shave all angels, including Mr Gold. Suki shave all clients too. Suki expert. I promise you enjoy.'

Shit. That my own pussy tingled in response didn't escape me.

Jonathon

I returned to the couch and touched the spot where she'd been, still warm, her sweet scent in the air, on me. I breathed it in and tasted it. It was beautiful. *She* was beautiful.

Normal procedure was underway now. The client would be horny and a little nervous. Suki would serve the client's favourite drink.

Emma Jane, she loves champagne. I smiled at the rhyme. Champagne suits her. They'd talk, laugh, relax, before the client showered and the horniness would bloom. Then Suki would shave her, before dressing her and leading her to the room of my choice.

I'd chosen the Round Room. I'd talk her through how the room worked, its external corridor and two-way mirrors, how tomorrow, strangers would touch her in the dark while she was shackled, and how I would be there at the end, waiting. Waiting to fuck her on the sunken bed. Normal procedure to maximise the client's enjoyment.

But Emma Jane wasn't a normal client. I'd made her come, on the couch. A first for me. And the smell of her musk, perfectly sweet, her nervous giggle and those smouldering eyes. No, this wasn't normal at all. I knew what I had to do. I picked up the phone, hoping I wasn't too late.

Emma

I tried objecting again, but it was all false bravado, and I guessed from Suki's raised eyebrow that she knew I'd already caved. I showered in a state of dreamy nervousness, the jets turned low, the water hot and steaming. I thought about what Suki was about to do to me and allowed the arousal; allowed it to flourish as I washed myself. This was a different world. I heard the phone ringing. Three rings and Suki picked up. I wondered who it was. Aunt Fee ringing to see if everything was okay?

Aunt Fee, the little minx. Suki would have shaved her, too. In my mind I saw her lying on her back with a cig in her mouth and reading a book while Suki got busy between her legs. If Aunt Fee could do it, so could I. I turned the water off.

Six

I poked my head from the shower and glanced through the archway into the bedroom area. I couldn't see Suki, so I stepped from the shower and wrapped myself in a fluffy white bathrobe, before quickly towelling my hair. I was going to do this, march right in there, ask her where she wanted me and open my legs for her. Shit, I was getting the shakes. What if I got turned on? Of course I'd get fucking turned on. I was already fucking turned on. What if she touched . . . where she shouldn't? What if I got carried away and pushed onto her fingers and my wildest fantasy became a reality? Fucking hell, this was crazy. I'd half a mind to jump back in the shower, but that would only prolong the agony.

I took a calming breath and checked myself in the mirror. I looked how I felt, hot and horny and a bit pissed. Red face, big eyes, and damp hair a mad nest. I put a smile on my face, raised my chin a little. You can do this, Emma Jane Winters. Just march right in there and spread your legs. Go!

And so I did. I dumped the towel in the sink, tightened the belt on the bathrobe, and I marched right in there.

I stumbled in shock when I saw him. He was sitting in the chair by the dresser, a glass of champagne in each hand.

'I'm sorry, I didn't mean to startle you.' He got to his feet.

My heart was in my mouth as I took the glass he offered. 'A toast,' he said.

'A toast?'

'Yes, I'd like to raise a glass to . . . to perfection.'

Our glasses touched with a clink. 'Perfection?' I withdrew my shaking hand quickly, clasping it still with the other. He took a drink of champagne and I gladly did the same.

He picked up the bottle and moved to the leather sofa where he sat and patted the seat beside him. 'Come.'

Jonathon

She joined me on the sofa. I could tell she was aroused, the flush down her neck, the dilated pupils; the rise of her chest and the catch of her breath. She took another drink of champagne and eyed me nervously. I wanted to undo the belt on her robe and free her breasts, wanted to touch, hold, caress. But no. All in good time.

'I always strive to give my clients an exceptional experience,' I said. 'In the beginning, I have a normal procedure that seems to work well. Would you like to know what that normal procedure is?'

She nodded, took another sip of champagne.

'I interview the client, on the couch, and I learn their desires and their fantasies, before sending them to be shaved by Suki, and then I fuck them in one of the fantasy rooms, and they always enjoy the experience.'

'Where is Suki?' she asked.

'I had to send her away,' I said and I'm certain I saw a flicker of disappointment in her beautiful eyes. I lifted one leg under me and turned to face her, my knee almost touching her robed thigh. 'Emma Jane, I don't normally finger-fuck my clients before they've had time to breathe. I don't normally touch them at all. And after you'd gone, when I should have been showering and changing and getting ready to fuck you in the fantasy room, I remained by the couch, thinking about you, and . . .' I drank my champagne in one and refilled our glasses.

'What fantasy room?' she said with a nervous edge to her voice. 'Are we going there now?'

'No,' I said firmly and her eyes smouldered before she looked away. 'Stand for me.'

She emptied her glass in one long swallow and I noticed the slight tremble in her hand. She placed the glass on the floor and got to her feet. I allowed slow seconds to pass before finishing my champagne and placing my glass next to hers. She looked nervous, flushed; and I was already getting hard. I got to my feet and her breath hitched as I reached for her. My hands rested on her shoulders and she visibly melted at my touch, her breathing now heavy. I pulled her to me and held her and her arms came around my waist and she held me back. The feel of her robed body against mine gave me a thrill I wasn't used to. I kissed her damp hair, then her warm brow before stepping back from her.

I took her hand and led her to the bottom of the bed nearest the archway and sat her down. 'Lie back for me, Emma.' She did as I asked, pulling her robe closed over her thighs as she settled.

I left her like that while I drew hot water into a shaving bowl. I soaked a towel and found a can of shaving foam and a razor. When I returned she'd relaxed a little; her legs were slightly open, her hands clasped on her stomach. I brought the chair from the dresser and placed the bowl and the other things on it. Then I took a step back from the bed.

'You look beautiful,' I said. 'Really beautiful.'

'Thank you,' she said.

'*Sir*, Emma. Call me, *sir* when you address me.'

'Yes, sir,' she said.

'Good girl. Now, I want you to bring your legs up, so that your heels touch your bottom.'

There was a slight hesitation but she did as I asked.

'Good. Now let your legs fall slowly open, as slowly as you can.'

Again a hesitation, and her legs were trembling, but she slowly let them fall open to reveal her pussy, inflamed and engorged, a hint of wetness at the folds of her lips. The dark pubic hair was not thick; it would not take long to shave it all away, but I would take my time, and she would feel every touch.

I picked up the damp towel and dunked it in the bowl of hot water. She flinched at the sound and my cock twitched in response. 'Your pussy is also beautiful,' I said, wringing the flannel into the bowl, the splashes and drops of water made her gasp.

'Thank you,' she said then gasped again as I pressed the hot flannel onto her pussy. I applied slight pressure and rocked my hand back and forth, just a little, and she gave an appreciative moan.

I shook up the can and squirted a generous pile of foam onto my fingers. She watched as I massaged the foam into both hands, and closed her eyes as I peeled the hot towel away from her pussy.

I touched all my fingers to her at once and smoothed the foam across her lips and up onto her pubic hair, massaging it slowly into a lather, and as I did so her legs unfolded either side of me and she moved against me.

'Good girl,' I said, increasing the pressure slightly against her slippery folds. I wanted to slide two fingers inside her right then, and had to take my hands away to restrain myself. 'Wider,' I said and she splayed her legs wide. 'That's perfect, Emma.'

I swished the razor through the hot water, then made the first delicate scrapes, holding the flesh still with the fingers of one hand as I brought the razor across her pubic area, small strokes, across and then downwards to her lips and she gasped as I pressed her lips to one side.

Now the other side and she moaned as I pushed her folds the other way and shaved away the fine hairs. I wiped away the excess foam with the towel and her ass left the bed as I rubbed her down. 'That's good, Emma Jane. Good girl.' Her hands were now at her sides, clasping the bedcover. She looked simply gorgeous.

As gently as I could, I stroked the razor over her pubic bone, going with the natural direction of the hairs, first one way then the next, and I returned to her lips, this time taking each lip between my fingers before pulling it to one side. She tensed and groaned each time and then I gave her pussy a final wipe down before stepping back.

'Touch your pussy,' I said, 'tell me how it feels.' As her hands came to her pussy, she brought her legs closed. I caught her by the heels. 'I did not say you could close your legs. Open them wide. I want to see you touch yourself.'

No hesitation this time. She opened her legs and ran her fingers over her pussy. 'How does it feel, Emma?'

'It feels . . . it feels sensitive, sir,' she said, in a breathy whisper. 'So sensitive.'

'Spread your lips for me, Emma.'

She held her lips apart, revealing glistening pinkness. 'Hold still,' I said.

Emma

'Hold still,' he said, and my God, I could feel the ache so bad; my pussy, so smooth and warm and inflamed from his touch. I wanted him inside me.

'Look at me,' he said.

I kept my pussy held open and stared at the man standing between my legs. He unbuttoned his shirt and shrugged it off revealing dark nipples and a toned torso. No sign of the tattoos Aunt Fee mentioned but shit this guy was hot and I was on show, waiting in anticipation for what might come next. My mouth was open, my breaths almost panting.

He came forward, slid his hands under my ass and lowered his head to my pussy. A long moan escaped me as his tongue ran a slow circle around my stretched lips. Then he pushed it inside and I shuddered, pulling my hands away to grip the bedcovers. I could feel every movement, and the beginnings of an orgasm pushed at my clit from within. 'Fuck me, please fuck me,' my words came out in a low whisper, then a groan as he pulled his tongue free and sucked at my lips, running my folds through his teeth and flicking his tongue at my clit. 'Oh God, fuck me, sir, just fuck me.'

One of his hands pulled away from under my ass and two fingers filled me up. I pushed onto them with a groan, 'More,' I said, and he obliged; three fingers now, stretching me as he twisted in and out. 'Fuck me,' I said again and his hands were taking mine and pulling me into a sitting position.

He walked to the archway and stopped to look at me. Maybe he was considering his next move. I wanted to jump him. Wanted to ditch the bathrobe and tear his pants off. Wanted to . . .

'Tell me what you want, Emma Jane.'

I took a breath. 'I really want fucking, sir. Like now.'

'Stand.'

I got to my feet.

He went to the dresser, rummaged in a drawer, came out with a sleep mask. He tossed it to me. 'Put this on.'

I put the mask on, relieved he could no longer see my eyes.

I heard him move, sensed his presence close. I opened my mouth to speak then thought better of it.

'What is it, Emma?' He was right in front of me.

I wanted him to hold me in his arms again. I wanted to feel him against me. 'Nothing, sir.'

'Are you sure?'

'Yes, sir.'

'Good. Take off your robe.'

My breasts tingled at his words and I could feel my nipples tightening. Grateful for the blindfold, I undid the belt and let the robe fall open before pushing it back off my shoulders. I shivered as it slid down my back to the floor.

His hands, warm and gentle, came to rest on my shoulders and I moaned as his fingers trailed down my chest and over my breasts, stopping to caress and gently tweak my nipples. A warm breath and his lips were at my right nipple, sucking it into his mouth, grazing, tugging. Oh God, I wanted him to fuck me so bad.

He moved to the other nipple, his hands at my back, pulling me onto him as he sucked and I groaned again at the waves of pleasure flowing through my tummy. My hands went to his head, fingers through his hair, forcing his face into my breast, and he didn't stop me. I worked against him as he sucked and nibbled and teased until eventually he broke free and came up for breath.

He took my hands and touched them to the front of his bulging trousers. He was big and hard as hell. He pressed my fingers to his belt buckle and then his hands were back to my shoulders. I fumbled at his belt and got it open and the zipper down. I gently freed his hard cock and held it in both hands.

'Tell me how it feels, Emma Jane,' he said, his tone laced with desire.

I cupped his thick cock in one hand and stroked it with the other. It was smooth and warm and velvety, and I could feel one bulging vein running its length. The urge to rip my blindfold away was strong. 'It feels . . . it feels really good, sir.'

'Really good? Is that all? Can you feel how hard I am?'

I could; he was as stiff as an iron bar. 'Yes, sir.'

'You make me horny, Emma Jane. Squeeze my cock and tell me how it feels.'

I gripped his cock with both hands and squeezed it and felt it stiffen further. 'It feels like fucking heaven, sir. Please fuck me.'

He broke away from me. I heard him kicking away his trousers, removing his boxers. Then silence, only our breathing.

My heart was beating so hard, my senses tingling for him. My breath caught as his warm hands touched to my shoulders once again. He pulled me into him, my head to his chest, his cock pressing into my tummy. I wanted to lift a leg and slide onto him.

'On your knees,' he said and his hands were guiding me as I slid down his body. His stiff cock ran up between my breasts and slapped at my chin. I ran my tongue under it to the tip and opened my mouth to take him in but he moved away.

'Suck,' he said and his balls were at my mouth. Smooth and tight. I sucked one in, gently, and loved it when he groaned. I took hold of his solid thighs and moved my mouth to the other side, applying more pressure this time, tugging a little as he groaned again.

'Both,' he said and the hardness of his shaft pressing into my nose made me want to suck him and fuck him so bad. I opened my mouth wide, desperate to please him. He pushed against me, tensing. 'Suck, suck hard, Emma.' His balls filled my mouth and I sucked. He laced his hands behind my head and pressed my face into his stiffness.

'Harder!' he said, his legs tensing against me. I sucked harder until he gasped and pulled away.

'Touch me, Emma,' he breathed.

I reached out slowly, tentatively, until my fingers touched to his thighs. I found his stiffness, curving upwards, veins prominent. I wanted to see it, wanted to rip my blindfold off and devour it.

'To your feet,' he said and his hands were under my elbows, helping me to my feet. 'Hands on your head.'

I did as he said and my breasts lifted and ached for his touch. I heard him moving, and soon his warm breath on the back of my neck confirmed he was behind me. He kissed me there, once, then again, making me shiver and the hairs on my neck prickled. I moaned as his hands touched to my waist, and slowly he ran his hands up to my breasts, cupped them, squeezed them gently, tugged at the nipples. My head fell back against his shoulder and I moaned with pleasure.

'What do you want?' he whispered in my ear, his stiff cock pressing against my ass.

What did I want? I wanted him to fuck me until I screamed.

'Tell me,' he said and squeezed my breasts hard. I gasped and buckled and he kept me upright and squeezed again.

'I want . . . I want your cock, sir.'

He let go of my breasts and turned me to face him. His hands took hold of mine still on top of my head and he placed them around his neck. Then his hands were at my sides, big strong hands. He lifted me and I wrapped my legs around his waist.

I sank my head into his shoulder and breathed in his musky scent. 'Please fuck me,' I said and at those words I felt the tip of his cock at my pussy and he moved me ever so slightly against it and my lips were parted. I groaned with desire as it stretched my opening and I gasped when the swollen head of his cock pushed into me.

'Squeeze it,' he whispered into my ear, so I clenched my pussy and his teeth scraped my neck. 'Again, do it again, squeeze it and hold it.'

I squeezed my pussy muscles so hard I felt the end of his cock twitch. I wanted to slide onto it, wanted it to fill me up.

'Put your arms out to your sides and lean back,' he said.

I let my arms out slowly and leaned back into thin air, his big hands holding me by the waist, and he allowed me to lower, just a little, onto his lovely fat cock. 'Oh God,' I moaned. 'I want you so much.'

And he slid it right in, and fucked me, slowly at first, my pussy tight around his thickness, my heels digging into the backs of his thighs, my arms hanging free as he pushed all the way in, filling me deep.

He moved one hand to my back and his mouth found my right nipple, and he sucked as he slowly fucked me, and the slickness down there was just perfect. He moved to my other nipple and sucked until my tit was filling his mouth and he bit down as he pumped me and I went with it, feeling the beginnings of the orgasm pulling at me from within. 'Fuck me hard,' I said, 'Please, sir. I need it fucking hard.'

We fell onto the bed and I was on top of him, straddling him, my tits hanging against his chest. He took hold of my hips. 'Be still,' he said, and I stilled, panting, waiting with his dick twitching inside me.

His grip tightened and he shuffled his ass into position and thrust into me and pumped me, faster and faster until the sucking burn made me shudder and buck and beg for more.

He pumped me so hard I fell forward and pressed my cheek against his chest and moaned and groaned as his cock did not stop, did not slow, and it felt so fucking wonderful.

'I'm gonna come. I'm gonna come,' I said and he stopped and

pushed me up from his chest.

'Ride me,' he said. 'Ride me, Emma Jane.'

So I did. I fucked that slicked up cock like a dirty girl and he banged me right back until my wetness was slapping and my tits were bouncing. My hands gripped his pecs and I was warbling for sweet Jesus and I thought my head would explode until the orgasm ripped through me, through us; I felt him let himself go and he thrust with each spasm, so hard and forceful that my knees left the bed and I cried out, my cries matching his grunts as he emptied himself inside me.

I collapsed on top of him, hauling in breaths, shaking and trembling all over. He eased me to one side and held me there, pulled me to him and our breaths joined as one, slowly calming, slowly melting.

'That was a wonderful ride,' he said. I raised my head towards his voice and his lips touched mine and he held them there, but only for a moment.

'Thank you,' I said when his lips left mine. 'Can I take the blindfold off now?' I so wanted to see him; see his firm naked body.

'No, you cannot.' He sighed and his fingers stroked through my hair. 'I have a treat lined up for you. A treat you will enjoy.'

'The fantasy room?'

'No, not yet. That will be tomorrow.'

'I'm intrigued,' I said. 'Please tell me more.'

There was a long pause before he spoke again. 'I decided the perfect fantasy room for you would be the round room.'

'A room that's actually round?'

'You'll have to wait and see.'

Now I really was intrigued. 'Please tell me.'

'No, you forgot to say *sir*, otherwise I might have.'

I smiled at his tease. 'I like being your sub, *sir*,' I said.

'And I like my dirty girl.' He kissed me again and then pulled away and the bed dipped and lifted as he got off it.

I heard him moving around, picking up his clothes. 'Sir?'

The door clicked open. I felt a slight draught and the door clicked shut.

'Sir?'

I took the sleep mask off.

I was alone.

Chapter Six

Scream if you wanna go faster

Emma

I was drifting on a tranquil cloud of sleepy bliss, stretching out on the covers before curling back up again and breathing in his heady scent. Images ran over and over in my mind. Me, a shuddering wreck on the couch as he'd pushed and pulled at my pussy. Him, appearing from nowhere and shaving me bare. Picking me up with little effort and fucking me in his arms, me with my arms spread wide like I was riding the fucking Titanic. Filling me deep as I rode him like a bucking horse . . . and the orgasm, so intense it burned through me like a firework going off and it hurt so insanely good I wanted more. I could feel his cum dribbling from me and I felt so content. *I like my dirty girl* I heard him say and I loved that. I was warming to the idea of being *his* dirty girl – *his* dirty sub. And this was only day one. I couldn't imagine what might be in store for me, what new heights he might take me to.

He'd mentioned a fantasy room – the *round room.* I wondered what that would entail. All I could picture in my mind was a round bed inside a round room. But what was the fantasy? Would it spin, like a fairground ride, and we'd fuck as we spun? *Scream if you wanna go faster*, hell yeah, I'd fucking scream all right. Jesus that man was hot.

I could just imagine spinning and fucking, deeper and deeper and so much fucking deeper. And now the fairground ride was a carousel, with *golden* horses, of course, and there was Jonathon, naked on the horse by my side. I'm climbing onto his horse, and he's holding me in his strong arms and fucking me from behind as the carousel turns and the horse bobs up and down. I realise my hand has wandered to between my legs and I'm circling my clit with sticky fingers. The faint thrum of tingles makes me moan and I spread my legs. I have the crazy thought – dirty thought – of licking my fingers clean. Somehow I knew Jonathon Gold would approve.

A knock at the door. I jumped upright and pulled the covers over me.

Suki walked in with a grin on her face. She was holding her little case in front of her.

'Jesus, Suki,' I said, breathless.

'Sorry, Miss Emma. Were you asleep?'

I think she knew I'd been anything but asleep. My flaming pussy was lighting up my face. 'No. I was just about to shower.'

'Good.' She placed her case on the dresser. 'Quick shower, quick cup of tea, then special treat.' With a sparkle in her eye, she whipped off her polo shirt, stepped out of her skirt and stood naked before me.

My heart was thumping. 'Treat?'

Suki nodded excitedly. 'Yes, Miss Emma, special spa treat, just for you and me, to help you unwind and prepare your body for . . . for next time with Mr Gold.'

'Oh?'

'Yes. And rules for spa is shower before entering.'

'I see.'

'Me and you have super relaxing time, Miss Emma.' She held out a hand.

I went with the flow. We showered together in the huge shower. Suki kept her distance. She also kept her eyes to herself, although I couldn't help but glance at her tiny body now and again. I'd never looked at another woman in the shower before, not like this.

We drank Suki's special tea as we dried off. She sat on the bed opposite me, wrapped in a huge fluffy towel. She looked so cute. And she still had that sparkle in her eye, as if she had a secret and wanted to blurt it out but couldn't. 'Are you okay?' I asked. 'You seem a bit . . . I dunno.'

She giggled in response.

'You're hiding something,' I teased.

She shook her head. 'Miss Emma, Suki hide lots of things.'

I pushed for more but she fobbed me off with confidentiality agreements and how all angels have to keep secrets from clients otherwise the client's fun might be spoiled. Hmm. I didn't quite believe her.

She went to the dresser and took from her little case a golden bikini. She removed the towel, patted herself down, and put the bikini on. I'd brought two bikinis, one sky-blue, the other tangerine. I went for the sky-blue, and we wrapped ourselves in fresh white bathrobes.

Jonathon

The sound of a door closing followed by happy chatter brought my eyes open. Suki and Emma heading to the spa. I was lying on my back on the bed in room 5, where I'd escaped to, clutching my clothes like a guilty teenager. I must have been here a while, basking in her sweet scent, reliving the taste and feel of her.

I was breaking all the rules, interfering with proven protocol, but it felt good – it felt real. I wondered which rule I'd break next. I thought about joining them in the spa, sending Suki away again, and we'd fuck in the hot pool and then fall into the icy plunge pool and she'd shriek in my arms as the water froze us through. Then I'd wrap in her in a warm robe, run my fingers through her tangled hair, enjoy the needy press of her gorgeous lips against mine, fresh and intoxicating . . .

I caught myself, sat up, swung my legs to the floor, and realised I had a hard on.

Emma

The spa turned out to be a separate building set among the gardens at the rear of the mansion; two levels, all arches, stairs, and huge windows strung with soft lighting – from the outside it looked like something from a fairy tale.

Once inside, Suki pressed a button on a wall panel and the place lit up. A rectangular swim pool with steaming water and a kidney-shaped icy plunge pool were separated by a line of three raised Jacuzzis. And the scent in the air was lovely – jasmine, I think.

Suki made straight for the well-stocked bar at the rear and made us both a *Slippery Nipple* – Baileys and Sambuca – her favourite, she said.

'Will Mr Gold be joining us?' I asked.

Suki placed our drinks on a table next to two loungers by the pool and proceeded to take off her robe. 'No, Miss Emma, this is just you time, to relax aching muscles. You do have aching muscles?'

Now she mentioned it, I did ache, just like I always did after a good ride. I smiled at the memory.

'Let me guess,' Suki said placing a finger to her chin and looking me up and down. 'Your thighs feel like tree trunks, your boobs as tender as leaves that are about to fall, and your pussy feels like you used a log for a dildo. Yes?'

I laughed and my laughter echoed around the high ceilings. Suki laughed too, and jumped into the pool. I took off my robe and joined her. The water was warm, soothing, and we swam a few slow lengths, the aches easing by the second. Floating on my back, staring up at soft purple lighting, I thought of getting my own pool installed at home, but reality came thudding back and slapped me in the face. The home I'd known all my life would soon no longer be my home; Emma Jane Winters would become Emma Jane Ripley, and William Ripley's pad was, of all things, an old vicarage. Good God. I laughed at the sentiment.

'What's funny?' Suki was treading water by my side.

'This,' I said, 'this place. I just love it.'

'Ever tried a plunge pool?' she said with a grin.

We exited the pool by the steps next to the Jacuzzis and went to stand at the edge of the plunge pool. I could feel the chill coming off the water. Both of us were steaming – like horses on a winter's day, I thought, and had a sudden pang for Gem and the gang back at the stables. There was no room at the vicarage for horses, either. What stupid mess was I getting into?

'Miss Emma?'

I blinked back to the moment and a shiver ran through me.

'It really cold,' Suki said. She took my hand. 'Ready?'

I nodded. Suki jumped and I jumped with her.

Jonathon

I'd showered, soon turning the water to cold and standing under it with my hands on the wall and my head bowed when I couldn't shake her from my mind. I'd dressed smart, suit pants and shirt and a splash of cologne, then I'd marched to the round room to check that it was spick and span and in perfect working order. And now? Now I laughed. I laughed at myself, sitting at my desk, in the dark, glass of whisky in hand, staring at my new screensaver.

She was standing by the car, the sun on her auburn hair, smiling, looking almost in the direction of the CCTV camera. And she looked so beautiful. She had an aura about her, a cheeky presence. I liked her a lot.

I thought of her in the spa; imagined her in her bikini, relaxing, having fun with Suki, healing the aches of the day in preparation for the next. Normal procedure, of course.

I closed the computer down and knocked the whisky back in one.

Emma

The icy exhilaration – which felt like my skeleton had leapt from my body – was followed by a bubbling Jacuzzi. Suki sat across from me and we sipped on our Slippery Nipples.

'Did you enjoy first fuck?' Suki asked with a grin.

I'd realised by now that Suki always got straight to the point. 'Yeah,' I said, feeling my face warm, although I knew I was hardly in any position to feel embarrassed. I decided that straight-to-the-point was probably the best way. 'It was incredible. No, scratch that, *he* was incredible.'

Suki's leg touched against mine beneath the bubbling water.

'Guess what?' she said.

'What?'

She made that cute little giggle and her eyes sparkled. 'It gets better. Tomorrow will blow your head off.'

'The round room?' My heart skipped a beat. 'What happens? Does it spin? I have this weird idea it might.'

Suki shook her head. 'No spin, Miss Emma, but it will make you dizzy.' She giggled again.

'Tell me what happens, please?' I said in a begging tone.

'I'm not allowed to say, but is really fucking good.'

I laughed. I don't think I'd heard Suki swear before. She moved her legs so that they were between mine, touching beneath the water. Our eyes met and still she had that mischievous glint, as if she was aching to blurt something out, or maybe it wasn't that. Maybe she was aching for something else. I could not deny the feeling when her legs touched mine, a purposeful touch, and the slightest tickle of a thrill running through me. My eyes went to the nubs of her nipples, proud through her golden bikini, and I wondered what it would be like to take Suki's nipples into my mouth. Jesus. I stopped myself. I'd never had feelings for a woman before – not in a sexual way. I decided Suki's special tea might have something to do with it – that and the cocktails. 'What aren't you telling me?' I said, 'Does it hurt?'

Suki cocked her head to one side, 'Does what hurt?'

'The round room, whatever goes on in there. Please, give me a clue at least.'

She sighed, thought for a moment, 'Well, no, it doesn't hurt unless you want it to, and . . . it's more what goes on outside the round room that will really get you coming.'

'Tell me more. Please?'

She moved her legs to the outside of mine, lifted her feet and placed them against the ledge I was sitting on, one either side of me, almost touching me; her knees protruding from the water. She reached to the control knob and turned the bubbles off and the place echoed into silence. 'I'm not allowed to give anything away. But I can say that all angels get initiation in the round room.' And there was that cheeky I'm-hiding-something grin again. 'On my first go, I orgasm five time. Round room is really hot, Miss Emma, you will like it a lot.'

'Five orgasms? With Mr . . . with Jonathon?'

She wagged a finger at me. 'Wait and see.'

'You're a tease,' I said and she touched her feet to my hips. I realised that Suki was highly-charged, a little sex bomb, and that one reciprocated touch from me could spark something. She wanted it. She wanted me. She was grinning again. I took a sip of my cocktail; the creamy Baileys mixture was going down well. 'Tell me what you're hiding?'

'Hiding? I told you, all angels have secrets. It's against –'

'– the rules to tell,' I finished for her. 'I understand you can't spoil surprises for clients, but it's more than that. When you came to my room you were like the cat that got the cream and you were dying to shout it to the world. And you've had that grin ever since.'

She drank the rest of her cocktail and placed the tumbler on the side. 'Okay,' she looked straight at me, 'It's Mr Gold. I've never seen him like this before.'

'Like what?'

'Acting strange. Like he bring you off on couch – that never happen. And then send Suki away so he can do shave. That never *ever* happen. And then he fuck you straight after – that never happen, either.'

'So?'

She giggled. 'So . . . you know.'

'Know what?'

'Mr Gold . . . he has hots for Miss Emma.'

Hearing those words out loud made my tummy flutter and heat spread down to my pussy. Fuck! Yes, that's what they meant by having the *hots*. I wanted him now, wanted to be fucked in his arms all over again. 'That's ridiculous,' I said, sipping my cocktail and trying to ignore my crimson face.

'When are you getting married?' Suki said and I almost dropped my drink.

'What?'

'The ring you took off for safety, was engagement ring?'

Shit. 'Yes. Married. Soon,' I said. 'Actually,' a long sigh escaped me, 'next weekend.'

Suki's feet left my sides and she stood up. Water dripped from her bikini, her nipples proud, 'Wow! Next weekend? So this week is like sexy hen party?'

I laughed but it came out choked. 'Something like that.' I found myself staring at Suki's pale tummy, or rather staring straight through it; thoughts of my wedding dress being picked up in Italy, thoughts of William and his vicarage and a life tied to man I didn't even like, never mind love. The tears came from nowhere and I sobbed great wrenching sobs. Suki's arms came around me and I cried into her shoulder.

Jonathon

I'd gotten as far as the spa's double doors before I managed to stop myself from breezing in there like a prize tool. Even though I still very much wanted to dismiss Suki and wrap myself up in Emma Jane. *Keep it professional*, I told myself.

Through the crack in the double doors I listened to every word, and the two girls had seemed happy and having fun. But Emma Jane was getting fucking married.

Suki stood up, said something about this being her hen party and Emma burst into tears. Suki hugged her, held her tight. My heart was racing.

I took my hand away and the door clicked shut.

Chapter Seven

The Loveseat

DAY TWO

Emma

I was in a dark church. A choir was singing. Bells were ringing. And I was gasping for breath, desperate to find a way out. But there was no door, only windows, and each window I ran to was barred with thick steel. *Dearly beloved*, said a loud resounding voice, *we are gathered here today . . .*

I woke in a sweat, heart rocking, and there on the dresser reflecting the dim blue backlighting, was my engagement ring.

04:20 the clock on the side said.

I took a breath. I'd declined Suki's offer to stay the night; now I wished she was here. I turned away from the dresser and cuddled one of the pillows. I'd cried myself to sleep thinking about what I had to do for the sake of the family. What I had to do, to keep Daddy happy and the family business healthy, strengthening his connections, boosting his already obscene bank account by marrying William *fuck-me-on-a-Friday* Ripley. Well, screw William Ripley, for now at least. I was going to put my impending doom out of my mind and have myself some fucking fun.

Jonathon

I eventually gave in and got up. It was only six a.m. when I rang Suki, but she came to my room with a spring in her step and her special tea in her little case. She said she hadn't slept well, was too excited about Emma Jane experiencing the round room, but after what I'd heard last night I was no longer convinced the round room should go ahead. I decided not to let Suki know of my uncertainty and kept up the pretence, at least for now.

Suki made us tea, and she sat on my bed as I explained what I wanted her to do from start to finish, no detail spared, how today had to be the absolute best for Emma Jane.

'Nothing but the *absolute* best,' I reiterated.

'Every step of the way, Mr Gold,' Suki said with a grin.

'Thank you, Suki. You always do an excellent job.'

She placed her cup on the side and stood to attention. 'Can I get you anything before I go?'

It took a few moments for the penny to drop; the fact she was staring at my crotch, concealed by the bedcovers, made it obvious. She really was an angel, but I wasn't feeling the mood. 'No thank you,' I said and her face dropped.

'Of course, sir,' she said and bowed out of the room.

I pulled on my sweats and a black tee and made my way outside and to the building that housed the round room.

I took hold of the shackles that dangled from the slot in the ceiling and walked through the strips of beading that curtained the first doorway. The shackles moved freely and smoothly on the rail. Of course they did. I walked the curved corridor, just as Emma would if this went ahead, and once inside the round room I tested the pulley system and made sure the shackles rose and fell smoothly because if this went ahead the beautiful Emma Jane would be hitched to the ceiling.

Hitched? *She's* getting hitched all right. And that's what's fucking bugging me. I left the shackles behind and went outside for air. The round room experience was meant for experienced clients of a perverse nature – and that meant every client. Normal clients signed up for pain and filth. But Emma Jane wasn't a normal client. Emma Jane wasn't experienced at all. Her being here was nothing more than an extravagant gift from a friend who hadn't put much thought into it. Putting Emma Jane through the round room might just . . . might what? Hurt her? Disgust her? No, it wasn't that at all, was it? I was being protective of her. I was getting involved. And getting involved was not something Jonathon Gold ever did. I leaned against the wall and watched a magpie on the lawn swallowing a worm. Emma Jane was beautiful. And sweet. And innocent. Emma Jane wasn't meant for the round room, or this place. I had to put a stop to this.

Emma

When I next woke it was Suki knocking on the door. She ran straight up to me and gave me a tight hug. 'Tea first,' she said, her infectious grin so wide I couldn't help smile back.

As we drank our tea, Suki explained what would happen before and after the round room experience. After, I'd be with my mentor relaxing in the spa, which I looked forward to. But before, I'd be breakfasting with Mr Gold himself. *That* made my stomach churn.

I was allowed a shower but no deodorant or perfume; it was

important that only natural scents came through for the perfect round room experience, Suki told me. So I was going to stink at breakfast? Great! Next, she produced a strapless summer dress in pale blue. It came to just above my knees and the elasticated top was snug above my boobs. It felt great with no underwear.

'You look lovely, Miss Emma,' Suki said, although I felt naked with no makeup. My heart was already banging and we hadn't even left the room yet.

She linked my arm and took me through the house to a huge conservatory, most of which was angled glass walls overlooking the lawns where the sun was shining. And there was Jonathon, sitting at a round table lit up by sunlight. His tight black tee showed off his perfect muscles, as did his denims tight to his thighs. I noticed he was barefoot, like me, and truly I could have jumped him, if he didn't look so stern.

'See you later,' Suki said and left me standing there like a kid before the headmaster.

He gestured for me to sit. No words just a curt nod. If he was trying to make feel like a submissive, he was doing a good job from the off. I knew I'd do anything he asked. *Anything*.

I took the seat opposite him. The chair scraped on the tiles when I pulled it in and I cringed but his stare didn't falter, even when I offered my best smile.

We were served eggs benedict, coffee, chocolate croissants, and chilled orange juice by an angel named Harry. I didn't have much of an appetite; my stomach was in knots thinking of what might be to come, what he might do to me, but I knew I needed to eat something. I started on the eggs benedict.

'This is really nice. Thank you,' I said. Jonathon drank his coffee.

I noticed he wasn't eating. 'Is there something wrong?'

Jonathon

I put my cup on its saucer a little too harshly and she flinched at the clatter. *Something wrong? I wanted to fuck you like a filthy dirty whore, but now I can't*, were the words flying around my head. 'You're getting married,' were the words that came out.

'Yes. Yes, I am,' she said. 'Is that a problem?'

She looked stunning in the pale blue summer dress I'd chosen. Her nipples were proud, and her cheeks flushed a little. I noticed her chest rising and falling and the glint of worry in her lovely eyes. Is there a problem? Where to start? What to tell? How much to say? 'This experience, Emma. I'm sorry, but I don't believe it's right for you.'

'Right for me?' She put down her knife and fork, picked up her coffee mug and held it with both hands in front of her, sipping from it. She looked a little guarded.

'Look,' I said, trying for a lighter tone. 'You're not . . . you're not . . .' I struggled for the right words.

She cocked her head. 'Not?'

'A normal client,' I said.

'I'm not?'

Now her cheeks were flushed. No, Emma Jane, you're not a normal client. I don't normally think of my clients every waking hour. I don't normally shoot my load in the shower while thinking of how many ways I'd like to fuck my clients. I could feel myself getting hard right now, for fuck's sake.

I took a drink of my coffee, placed the cup down gently. 'Quite simply, Emma, my clients are perverts. They dally with the harsher, filthier facets of sexual gratification. The round room experience I had planned for today is a perfect example. It's dirty, filthy, bare-knuckled sexual gratification, an experience my wealthy clients pay a lot of money for – perverse clients. Not a client with limited experience who's here for what really amounts to nothing more than an expensive hen party.'

Her eyes went wide, as did her lovely mouth. She looked hurt.

'But I want to experience it,' she said. 'This is why I'm here. To give me the experience, and to . . . to make me a stronger person. That's what Aunt Fee said. And I want that.'

'*Aunt* Fee?'

She looked down at her plate. 'Yes. She paid for this. Said it would be good for me.'

'Your generous friend, Fiona . . . is your aunt?' Now I could see the family resemblance.

'Yes, she's my aunt. Are you saying this is coming to a stop altogether? Or is it just the round room I'm not allowed to do?'

I decided the best action now would be to furnish her with some hard facts. 'Emma, listen to me. The round room is extreme. You will be shackled and blindfolded. Strangers will touch you. Male *and* female. They will nip you, bite you, finger you, abuse you until you come again and again. And when they're done with you and you're all filthy and sweaty, I will take you as mine and you will come so hard you will scream for mercy.'

I could barely believe it when she smiled at me. 'I don't see a problem,' she said with attempted confidence, but there was a nervous edge to her voice.

'Oh, there are problems all right. Rules are few for the round room. You could come out the other end with bites and bruises or worse. I now realise why your friend stipulated that you weren't to be marked. Obviously you don't want your *fiancé* to know what you've been up to.'

She sat up straight, looked me in the eye. 'Mark me, then. I don't care.'

'You don't care what your husband-to-be will think?'

'No, I don't. I want this. I want what you can do for me.'

'I don't think you can handle it,' I said, and felt like a twat.

She put her coffee down, wiped her mouth with her napkin. 'You will never know that unless you try.'

My cock was pushing at my jeans. I wanted to put her over my knee and spank some sense into her. 'If you don't care about what your fiancé might think, why the hell are you marrying him?'

She let out a sigh, placed her napkin on her plate. 'You want the truth?'

I nodded. 'Always.'

'Okay, then the truth is I don't want to marry him. I don't love him. I don't even like him. I have to do it for the family, to keep Daddy and Mummy rich and my *inheritance* in good order.'

'I see.'

'Do you? Do you really? Maybe you don't see at all. I *have* to marry William Ripley, no questions asked, it's been planned for years, and now the time is right because Daddy's shares will go through the roof. There's millions at stake. If I said *No*. If I even hinted at *No*, my parents would disown me and I'd lose everything. This week here with you, this gift from Aunt Fee, I'm having the best time and I want more of it. And if I go home with bruises I really couldn't care less.' Her eyes glistened with threatening tears.

'There's more to life than money, Emma. And more to life than doing the right thing to please others.'

'Try telling my parents that. Please, Jonathon. I'm doing this for me. Something for me for a change. I want what you can offer. And I know I'll leave here a better person. Please don't take this away from me.'

She got to her feet, clasped her hands before her. I noticed the slight tremble. 'I want to stay and experience what has been paid for. And I want the round room, *and* marking. You can hit me.'

I almost laughed at her naivety. 'I can hit you?'

'Yes. I want it. Do it now . . . *sir*,' she added.

'You aspire to be the good submissive, do you?'

'Yes, sir. Please, sir.'

Fine. If that was the way she wanted to play it. She didn't have a clue what she was asking for. And it was beautiful. Fucking beautiful. 'On your knees,' I said and she sank to her knees without hesitation. 'Eyes closed.' She closed her eyes.

I got to my feet and stepped up to her and noticed the slightest hitch of her breath. 'Open your mouth,' I said and she did. 'Wider,' and she stretched her mouth wide.

My dick was twitching for her. I wanted to feel those full lips around the end of my cock. I wanted to fuck her throat; wanted to free her gorgeous tits and splash them in cum, smear them, mark her as mine. But I resisted the urge. I touched a finger to her bottom lip and she closed her mouth and sucked my finger in, running her tongue around it and scraping her teeth back and forth. The blood was rushing to my cock. I pulled my finger away.

I touched my hand to her cheek; it felt as warm as it looked. 'You really want me to hit you, Emma Jane?'

Emma

I noticed he was using my second name again. 'Yes, sir.' His hand stroked down my neck to my bare shoulder and his touch made my nipples tingle and pucker.

'Wait here,' he said.

I kept my eyes closed and remained on my knees as his footsteps trailed away. What would he come back with? A whip? A cane? What the hell was I thinking? But I knew what I was thinking. I wanted this – I wanted *him*.

A hand on my shoulder and I jumped.

'Sorry, Miss Emma. Come this way please.'

She helped me to my feet and led me outside. 'Where are we going?'

Suki linked me, and pulled in close as we left the main path and crossed the lawn through leafy trees. 'Suki prepare Emma Jane for punishment,' she said.

'Prepare? Prepare how?'

'Mr Gold wants you in the loveseat,' she said, 'with ass in air,' she added.

Oh shit! We arrived at an archway in a redbrick wall draped with trailing ivy. Inside was a garden, blooming with all kinds of flowers; and there were trestles, gazebos, climbing roses, sunflowers, birds flitting and bees buzzing. A beautiful place. I was crapping myself.

In the centre of the garden was the loveseat; a wooden bench painted pale blue. It had a padded headrest, and huge carved wings spread out from behind – angel wings, like the mirror in the bathroom. In the middle of each wing was a heart-shaped hole – a nice touch, I thought.

Suki went behind the seat, and through each little heart-shaped hole she fed a chain with a shackle on the end. 'Kneel up onto seat please.'

I did as she asked, facing the wings, the wooden slats hard on my knees. Suki stepped up onto the bench and fastened the shackles around my wrists. She climbed down, went back behind the seat and the chains tightened until my arms were raised high and my stomach was pressed against the padded headrest.

'Comfortable?' she said when she reappeared at my side.

'Yes, I think so,' I lied.

'Good.' She stood up on the bench once more, lifted my dress and tucked the skirt into the elasticated band at my shoulders. 'Ass in air,' she said and climbed back down. 'I see you later, Miss Emma.'

And with that she vanished. And I waited. Strapped tight to wooden angel wings with the morning sun on my bare ass. I listened to the birds singing. I listened to the bees buzzing. I listened to my beating heart and to the pain in my knees from kneeling on the wood. This was anything but comfortable. I wondered how long he'd keep me waiting. Was this my punishment, burning in the sun with pained knees? The minutes ticked by. I rested my forehead against the wooden wings and tried to take some of the pressure from my knees. He was keeping me waiting on purpose. But that was part of the game, wasn't it? *Anticipation.* Well that was just fine, I'd wait all day if I had to. I'd do whatever it took to show Jonathon Gold that I deserved to –

'Remember when your nanny used to spank you?'

I jumped at his voice. He was right behind me and I hadn't heard him approach. And now he was staring at my bare ass. I clamped my thighs together.

'Answer me!'

I took a breath. 'Yes, sir. I remember.'

'And you used to like your punishment, didn't you?'

'Yes, sir.'

'Open.'

I edged my knees apart and could feel I was already getting wet down there.

'Wider. I want your knees as far apart as you can get them. Now!'

I shuffled my knees as far as they would go.

Silence. I could feel his eyes on me. I gasped when his hands touched to my ass and I gasped again when he parted my cheeks.

'Do you know,' he said. 'It is possible to orgasm from a spanking?'

My clit sparked at his words. 'No, sir. I didn't know that.' He slipped his hand under me and I moaned at his touch. Christ I was soaking wet.

'Do you deserve to be spanked?'

'Yes, sir.'

He pulled his hand away and appeared at my left side. 'Why? What have you done so wrong that you should be rewarded so?'

I looked into his gorgeous eyes. He wasn't smiling.

'Tell me, Emma Jane. Why should you be punished?'

What the heck was I supposed to say? 'I . . . I don't know, sir.'

He lifted one foot up onto the seat and slid his knee under my stomach, pushing my ass out further, the chains at my wrists pulling tight. He brought one hand to the small of my back. 'I will tell you why,' he said. I felt his leg tense against me and the smack came a moment later. I cried out, the hot sting on my ass was instant.

'You are a fool,' he said and brought his hand down again.

I yelped and forced his leg against the back of the seat and he held me there as he brought his hand down again and again.

'Six,' he said. 'Yes, six. Six of the best every time and you will come for me. Do you understand?'

'Yes! Yes, sir!'

Smack! Followed by five more and my ass was on fire.

'I called you a fool, Emma Jane. Why do you think I would do that?'

'I don't know, sir,' I said between breaths.

'Because,' he said, resting his hand on my burning ass, 'you are marrying someone you don't love, and that is a foolish thing to do, wouldn't you agree?'

I couldn't really argue. 'Yes, sir.'

Smack! Harder this time. And five more in quick succession made me writhe and wriggle against the wooden angel wings, my breasts scraping harshly, my pussy pulsing in time with the sting. Christ!

'Marrying for money is also foolish!' Smack, smack, smack, smack, smack, 'Foolish!' SMACK!

Jesus it fucking hurt.

His hand came to rest on my ass again. He applied pressure in a circular movement and my pussy tingled with desire. I got the feeling he was weighing up what to do next. I wanted his fingers, tried pushing against his hand. I wanted him to get up on the seat and fuck me hard.

Smack! He caught me by surprise and I screamed because he caught me good. Sting upon sting and I was writhing again. Smack! Followed by so many more I lost count and was on the verge of begging him to stop when the first pings of orgasm sprang from deep within.

'Tell me what you are,' he said, breathing heavily.

'I'm a fool!' I shouted. 'A sorry bloody fool!'

'Good girl,' he said. Smack! Six times. Hard. Fucking hard. I screamed at the last and the angel wings trembled at my thrashing.

His fingers slid down the crack of my ass and touched to my pussy. I was soaking fucking wet and desperate to come.

'Are you ready to come for me, Emma Jane?'

'Yes, sir,' I gasped. 'More than ever.'

Jonathon.

I braced my knee tight against her stomach and ran my hand over her beautifully pink arse. 'Come,' I said and smacked her arse dead centre. She bucked forward but I struck her again straight away and I didn't stop. I brought my hand down again and again as hard as I could and she cried out with each smack until the cries of pain turned to shrieks of bliss and she was trembling, quivering, grasping the chains and swaying against me and despite the ache in my wrist and the numbing feeling in my hand I picked up the pace and smacked her repeatedly until she screamed and fell away from me effing and blinding and gasping for breath.

I stood up, undid her shackles and, to her credit, she got straight to her feet, her eyes smouldering. 'Thank you, sir,' she said, her voice trembling and gasping for breath. 'Am I allowed the round room now?'

'Nothing's changed,' I said, resisting the urge to pull her into my arms. I couldn't put her through the round room. I just couldn't. It didn't feel right at all.

'Please,' she said, dropping the *sir*. 'This isn't a game, Jonathon. I've just been spanked. Severely spanked. So hard that you made me come and my ass hurts like fuck. I want more. However dirty you might think it is, this is the craziest thing I've ever done and I can fucking handle it.'

I was beginning to think she probably could.

'Please?' she repeated. 'At least let me try. And you'll be there, won't you? So nothing can go wrong?'

She'd given me an idea. Normally I wouldn't be there. Normally I'd be watching through the two-way mirrors as the client endured the attentions of many strangers. Normally. But again this was proving to be anything but normal. I could be there, right there with her. Another fucking rule broken.

'Jonathon?'

Now it was my turn to take a steadying breath. I moved behind her and she gasped when I slid my arms through hers and cupped her breasts. 'What is your favourite season of the year?' I breathed the words against her neck and she sank into me.

'Autumn. It's autumn; the falling leaves, the colours, I love autumn, sir.'

'Then that shall be your safe word.' I found her nipples through the cotton of her dress and squeezed them gently. She let out a soft moan and her head went back against my shoulder. 'Say it.'

'Autumn,' she said and it sounded so soft on her lips.

'Again!'

'Autumn, sir. Autumn.'

I took her nipples between thumb and forefinger and squeezed them again. 'My wish, Emma Jane, is that I never hear that word pass your lips again.' I loved that her breathing was heavy now, her breasts rising and falling in my hands. 'You have convinced me, Emma Jane.'

'I have?'

'Yes, you will experience the delights of the round room,' I squeezed her nipples again and tugged on them and she ground out a moan.

I released her nipples and squeezed her breasts hard. 'Does that excite you?' I let go of her breasts and she panted.

'Yes, sir. It excites me, sir.'

Chapter Eight

The Round Room

Emma

I was seriously turned on. With aching breasts and heat between my legs, and ass cheeks that felt like they were melting, I followed Jonathon Gold around to the rear of the house and there on the lawn in front of the spa building was a line of angels. They were exercising and all wore the standard white polo shirts and white skirt or trousers. I counted as we approached – twenty in all. My heart was suddenly pounding.

'The round room,' Jonathon gestured to a building to one side of the spa building; I hadn't noticed it last night in the dark. 'Come,' he said and I gladly followed to get away from the eyes of the watching angels.

The building was round, about twenty feet across, with a porch-like entrance. It looked a bit like an igloo but with a flat roof.

Inside the porched area, Jonathon opened a door and I stepped into a small space. To my right and to my left and also directly in front of me were beaded curtains. Hanging through a slot in the high ceiling was a chain and two leather cuffs. From a hook on the wall, Jonathon took what looked like a small remote control. He pressed a button and the chain lowered through its slot with a soft purr.

He strapped the cuffs around my wrists, pressed the remote and the chain retracted, pulling my wrists above my head.

'I won't give you the full stretch on the walk-through,' he said. 'My concern is for your shoulder. How does it feel?'

'It feels fine, sir,' I said, and it did feel fine.

'Good. Then let us begin. When I move this little lever,' he showed me the remote. 'The chain will move you forward or backward. And when I use these buttons the chain will lower or raise. In other words, I will be controlling your journey at all times. Understood?'

'Yes, sir.'

He turned me to my left, facing the bead curtain, and pressed the remote. The chain moved forward and I walked with it, through the curtain and into a narrow corridor, perhaps it was only four feet across.

The corridor ran ahead of me, curving to the right, and the slot in the centre of the ceiling ran with it. The wall on my left was painted blood-red, but the wall on my right was floor to ceiling mirrors all the way. 'You look so beautiful,' he said behind me, and I glanced at my reflection, arms raised, breasts pulled together, nipples showing through the blue cotton of my dress. Now I realised why I was wearing strapless.

He pressed the remote and the chain moved forward in the slot, taking me with it. Spotlights set into the ceiling to one side of the slot, lit our way.

'The next time you pass through this corridor you will be blindfolded,' he said, walking along behind me. 'And you will have the company of the angels you saw warming up out front.'

Fuck. My pussy pulsed at the thought.

'How does that make you feel, Emma Jane?'

'Horny, sir. Really horny.'

'Good,' he said as the corridor curved and a beaded curtain came into view. We'd come a full circle.

The chain pulled me through the curtain and then turned in its slot so that I was facing the middle beaded curtain, the one I'd faced when we first entered. He pressed the remote and I was pulled through the beads into a brightly lit room. The room was perfectly round and through its glass walls I could see the corridor we'd just walked through. Two-way mirrors. A neat touch.

He pressed the remote and the chain pulled me forward. The soft black covering I was now walking on was actually a bed, or a mattress of some sort. It filled the room at floor level and there was a scattering of blood-red cushions. Jonathon came to stand in front of me. He pressed the button to lower the chain and loosened the cuffs. The chain retracted and travelled back through the curtain behind me.

'I will control your journey through twenty naked strangers, and by the time you reach this point it will be just us, Emma Jane. And you will bring me release, yes?'

Hell yes, I wanted to say. *I want you to hold me in your arms and fuck my brains out again*, I wanted to say. *Just fuck me now*, I wanted to say. But I didn't. 'Yes, sir. I will, sir.'

'Then let us get started.'

Back outside the angels were stood in a line on the lawn. They stared at me and I stared back with my face on fire. Ten men and ten women. One woman stood out – a pretty black girl with a huge afro. *Sammy* her name tag said.

'Begin,' Jonathon said at my side and the angels whipped off their tops in unison, and all stepped out of their skirts and trousers. Twenty naked people. I'd never seen so much cock, or tits and pussy, and all of them shaven. I wished Suki was among them and suddenly I was buzzing again. This was really going to happen. My eye caught the black girl's. Her breasts were globes, the nipples black and round. She was smiling at me.

Jonathon snapped his fingers and the angels all turned and filed into the round building.

'Come,' he said, and he took my hand and it felt so nice even though my tummy was churning as we approached the building. 'Anticipation, Emma Jane. Remember what I told you?'

My mind was a blur. I couldn't remember at all.

'Foreplay,' he said as we stepped through the door and into the small space. 'Anticipation is foreplay.' He pressed the remote and the chain and cuffs lowered. He strapped my wrists into them and I took hold of the chain. With his free hand he hooked a finger into the elasticated top of my dress and pressed the remote again. The chain rose and pulled my hands high and the dress came down over my breasts and they sprang free, my nipples hard and aching to be touched. He slid the dress down and it pooled at my feet.

He turned me to the left once again and stood between me and the beaded curtain. Without another word, he pulled his tee off over his head and dropped it to the floor. He touched his fingers to my jaw and trailed them softly to my lips. From his pocket he took a blindfold and slipped it over my head. His hands came to cup my face and held me still. Then his lips touched to mine. A tender kiss. And I groaned into it, kissed him back with a pressure he didn't reciprocate. He let go of my face and stepped back.

I heard his belt unbuckling and his jeans coming off, then a draught as he passed me by. His hands touched to my shoulders. 'Are you ready, Emma Jane?'

Truly I was crapping myself. 'Yes, sir.'

The soft purr of the chains and I was pulled higher until I was on my toes and moving forward, the strings of beads touched to my breasts and flowed around me.

Three or four awkward steps and the chains went still. I listened intently but couldn't hear even a breath. The smell, though, was evident. Musk. The smell of arousal.

Soft lips touched to my right nipple and sucked it in and I yelped in surprise but soon I was moaning as my left nipple was sucked into another mouth. Two hungry mouths sucking and scraping and I didn't know if they were male or female but it felt so good that I moaned for more. The two mouths pulled away from me and the chain moved me forward, the two naked bodies brushed past me, the soft firmness of breasts passed across my ribs and the rush of tingles to my pussy made me shudder. I could hear Jonathon behind me, his breathing heavy.

A few more tiptoed steps and the chain stopped again. Big hands came to rest on my hips. More hands appeared at my feet and my legs were parted and lifted and for a moment I held my own weight on the chain before those big hands were cupping my ass and a hot mouth suddenly latched onto my pussy and sucked at my folds, tongue probing then licking its way up to my clit in quick strokes. This was a man; I felt the slight scrape of stubble as his tongue flicked at my clit. It didn't take long. I was coming, trembling, mewling like a dirty girl and loving every filthy fucking second.

'Good girl,' Jonathon said as my growls echoed down the corridor.

The man backed away and my feet were placed back to the floor and I was still writhing in the shackles as the chain pulled me forward a few tottering steps before it came to a halt once more. This time soft hands came to rest on my armpits. Warm breath against my lips. A gentle kiss there, and then a kiss to my chin, to my neck, and another to my shoulder before the wetness of tongue ran down to my nipple and I moaned into it, aching for more sucking. But no sucking came. The face that pressed into my breasts was smooth and warm, the frizz of hair that tickled my chest brought wetness trickling to my thigh. It was the black girl, Sammy. The chain above me whirred and her full breasts rubbed over mine as I was lowered. No words were spoken but I didn't need any encouraging. As a thick nipple passed over my chin I took it into my mouth and sucked it hard. The girl moaned and pushed into me, one hand on the back of my head. I found myself wishing my hands were free so that I could touch her all over and hell, that Jonathon was right behind me, watching, made it all the more horny and I felt so dirty. Both of Sammy's hands were at the back of my head now, pressing her full breasts into my face, my teeth scraping, nipping, biting and she was panting as her leg came up and over mine and she started rubbing her wet pussy back and forth on my thigh.

I felt the first pulse of another orgasm and gasped when she took one hand away and slipped it down between us. She was fingering me, two fingers, sliding through me with ease. I came straight away and so did Sammy, bucking onto my leg and I returned the pressure as she groaned and trembled. Jesus Christ Almighty and damn me to Hell and back. This was so fucking hot. So fucking horny. I was no longer crapping myself. I was officially a dirty girl and I fucking loved it.

'Enough,' Jonathon said and suddenly Sammy was gone and the chain whirred, taking me up on my toes and pulling me forward as hands touched and groped and it was bliss, my pussy on fire. The chain stopped, my feet swayed. Steadying hands caught my hips. Man's hands, I thought and was proven right when he pulled into me, his hard cock pressing into my tummy. He slipped a hand between us and forced his cock down and between my legs. 'Oh God,' I moaned as his hardness slid through the gap at the top of my thighs. He moved slowly forward, then slowly back, hands on my hips again, back and forth his cock glided through my wetness, teasing my lips apart but never penetrating.

'Fuck me,' I said in a whisper, arching into him, squeezing my thighs together, trying to catch the tip of his cock, trying to get it inside me. But the chain whirred once again and I was being lowered to my knees. The man grabbed my shackled wrists and held them to his chest. My lips found his cock and sucked him in and he fucked my mouth, my teeth scraping his shaft as he pulled out and pushed back in. I felt him tighten, knew he was going to come but he pulled away and again I was being lifted back to my toes and the chain whirred as I tottered, panting, aching for another release.

Then silence. I tried listening in the darkness but my own breaths were too loud. I waited, anticipating the next touch but none came. Anticipation is foreplay, yes it fucking is. A heartbeat and the chain whirred. I was being lowered slowly. Only this time it didn't stop. I was lowered all the way to the floor, on my knees, my shackled wrists held in front of me. I stared into the blindfold, waiting for a touch, a movement. I sensed it more than heard it; someone to the right of me, and now, someone to the left.

I jerked in surprise when a hard cock slapped against my lips, and then again when a second cock hit me on the cheek. I tried grabbing with my mouth but they were too quick, slapping their meaty dicks at my face. Hands now, at my knees, parting them, and the men at my sides took hold of my arms and lowered me to my back. The frizz of afro between my thighs sent a thrill quivering through me, then her full lips were at my pussy, sucking and licking.

'You're doing so well, dirty girl,' Jonathon said and I fucking loved it.

I groaned into it, writhed onto Sammy's hot mouth but the men at my sides stilled me. My head was lifted and a cock pushed into my mouth. Fingers at my lips spread my mouth wider and the second cock nudged into place and I did my very best to accommodate. Two cocks in my mouth at the same time might have been enough to bring me off again, considering the state I was in. But Sammy's expertise knew no bounds. As the first spasm of orgasm bucked me, she slid a wet finger up my ass and wriggled it and I almost choked on cock as I came and just at the right moment she yanked her finger away and I screamed a muffled scream of bliss. The cocks pulled away and so did Sammy and once again the chains lifted me to my toes.

'You're doing so well, Emma Jane,' came his voice laced with lust. Oh how I wanted his cock inside me.

I wondered if I was at the end now, and that the next thing to touch me would be the bead curtain, but no, the chain stopped moving. Hands on my legs, lots of hands front and back, and mouths kissing, tongues licking up my thighs to my ass, to my pussy. Soft hands parted my ass cheeks and a tongue tickled at my hole and it felt so nice. I groaned as the tongue pushed inside and the fingers holding me open dug into my cheeks and it felt so fucking good. I pushed onto the probing tongue at the same time as wandering fingers found my pussy and once again an orgasm simmered and sparked.

More closeness of bodies arrived at my front, touching, pressing. Kisses on my breasts and a mouth latched on to my right, then another to my left, and they sucked. God how they sucked as the tongue at my ass licked and probed. God how they fucking sucked as the fingers fucking my pussy pulled away to be replaced by a hard mouth. Stubble scratched my thigh as his mouth found my pussy, his lips pulling at my pussy lips, his tongue flicking at my tender clit. My whole body tensed and all at once I screamed out as the orgasm ripped from my tits to my hungry cunt and the four mouths devoured me as I pulled on my shackles. 'Jesus!' I said out loud, panting like a bitch in heat.

Then they were gone, and I could barely walk as the chain whirred and pulled me along. The beaded curtain flowed around me and I came to a stop, gasping for breath.

Sudden light as the blindfold was whipped away forced my eyes closed. I took a breath and slowly opened them, blinking to adjust to the light. The chain whirred and moved in its slot, turning me to face the final beaded curtain. I looked down at my breasts, red-sore and tender but throbbing for more attention. The chain whirred and I was lifted onto my toes, the stretching ache in my underarms almost too much to bear.

Through the strings of beads, the room beyond was in darkness. Don't leave me hanging, I thought as I waited for what might happen next, then I realised he would be able to see me under the dim light. He was watching, looking at my bruised tits and the glisten on my thighs. I rattled the chain, made sure he could hear how heavy my breaths were. I needed him inside me. Needed a good hard fucking.

The chain whirred and I was pulled through the bead curtain and my toes touched onto the soft mattress. The dim light from outside was just enough for me to see his shape in the darkness. He was lying on the bed before me, propped on his elbows.

'Emma jane,' he said and my heart fluttered at the sound of his voice.

'Sir,' was my throaty reply.

'You impressed me,' he said.

'Thank you, sir.'

'How do you feel?'

'Dirty, sir.'

'Good. Get ready, Emma. I think you might enjoy this.'

'Yes, sir.'

The spotlights outside in the corridor came on and the sight that met my eyes made my pussy weep; at least that's how good it felt. I was surrounded by angels, all of them fucking, all in different positions. One girl was being eaten out while doing a handstand. Another was sitting on a guy's face, working herself back and forth as she took his cock down her throat. Sammy, the black girl was directly in front of me behind Jonathon, her huge breasts squashed against the glass as the guy behind her slammed into her. A shouted grunt from my left and one guy erupted his cum over a blonde girl's face and she lapped it up. And amongst all this was Jonathon Gold and his perfect body, waiting just for me. Jesus, my juices were running down my legs.

'What do you want, dirty girl? Tell me,' said the brooding shadow on the bed before me.

'I want fucking. I want you to fuck me hard.'

'Sir!' he barked.

'Sir. Please. Just fuck me.'

The chain whirred and I yelped as I dropped suddenly, about a foot before the chain went taut and my arms pulled and fuck how they bloody ached.

'Open,' he said and I opened my legs like a willing slut.

My feet touched to his bare legs and I stepped over them as he pulled his legs together. The chain whirred and I was slowly lowered, my legs parting and bending at the knees until I came to a stop and I gasped as the tip of his cock touched to my pussy. He moved it back and forth, teasing my hot slit and I groaned in pleasure. I tried sitting onto it but the chains held me tight. 'Please sir. Please fuck me.'

'No,' he said and the mattress dipped as he shuffled forward. His hands came to my ass and his mouth made straight for my clit. He scraped it with his teeth and I jerked in the shackles but he stilled me with his hands and slipped three fingers inside me, soon followed by another, four thick fingers pummelled me into a frenzy as his tongue lapped and flicked at my clit.

The shackles took my full weight as I pushed into his face and turned to jelly as his fingers mashed me into a state of bliss where the world vanished and the only thing that mattered was the orgasm bursting from my dirty cunt. As the bodies in the corridor sucked and fucked I screamed and shuddered and bucked into his face and the final release came in a gush of wetness that startled me, and although I couldn't see it, I could hear it. I was squirting over his face and he was lapping it up and shit it fucking hurt as I bucked and writhed and screamed blue murder as the orgasm kicked through me like a shying horse.

'What the hell was that?' I gasped, panting for breath as it came to a stop.

The bed dipped as he pushed away from me. I could only just make out his form leaning back amongst the cushions. The lights in the corridor flickered and went off. I could hear movement, footfalls, then the beaded curtain outside as the angels departed. We were alone. Only my heavy breaths in the darkness.

The lights above me came on, so bright they forced my eyes shut.

'Look at me,' he said.

And there he was, all grin and dimples and sparkly eyes, his body toned and muscled, the sheen of my wetness down his chest, his legs spread, his dick standing proud, and the tattoos, flames of red, orange, and yellow licked around the V of his hips. And at the end of each flame was the head of a snarling dragon. His cock stood tall, the end engorged. Oh God. Never before had I wanted fucking so badly.

The chain whirred and once again I was hoisted to my toes.

'You are so beautiful,' he said.

So are you. 'Thank you, sir.'

The chain whirred and pulled me forward. I tiptoed up the bed until my feet came to a stop at his thighs.

'I need to come, Emma Jane.'

My pussy throbbed in response, 'Then fuck me, sir,' I said.

The chain whirred and lowered. He lifted my feet and placed them at his sides and slowly I came down but this time his cock didn't stop at my pussy lips. His hands came to my lower back as I slid onto him and the feel of his thickness stretching me sent my clit into overdrive and I moaned like a needy whore. I wanted him to release my shackles and hold me and fuck me, the need to come again so crazily hot.

As my knees touched to the bed either side of him and his cock came to rest buried deep within me, he loosened the shackles and I fell into him. He held me there, hugged me to him, and we locked together so perfectly.

My head on his shoulder, his mouth close to my ear, his warm breath so soothing, so nice. My pussy clenched involuntarily and as he groaned in response his cock twitched inside me. I could stay this way forever.

Jonathon

Gently, and without withdrawing, I rolled her to one side and moved on top of her. She let her arms fall to the bed, outstretched. She was sweaty, her damp hair a nest, her lovely tits bruised, the nipples taut and tender-looking, her lips so full and moist, and her pussy wrapped around me tightly; she was simply gorgeous.

I hitched up her knees and held her legs open, starting slowly, I withdrew until just the knob of my cock was inside her. As I pushed slowly all the way back in she moaned and lifted her ass to meet me.

'That's so good,' she said.

I touched a finger to her lips, and then I could resist no more. I kissed her. And she responded, sucking my tongue into her delicious mouth, her hands in my hair, her tight cunt squeezing at my cock. I bit her lip, kissed down her neck, took a nipple in my mouth and sucked it hard as she gasped and pulled my head into her.

'Fuck me, Jonathon,' she said.

And so I did. I hooked her legs over my shoulders and fucked her hard and fast until her sopping cunt was almost sucking inside out with the friction and my cock was feeling the beautiful ripping burn. Our eyes locked as I pummelled her and she grunted and puffed and I didn't stop, didn't slow, held my breath until her eyes rolled to the back of her head and her legs tensed around my neck and she yelled out her orgasm as my cock exploded inside her.

She bucked and writhed on the bed as I pulled away. I settled beside her and she curled into me. What a beautiful girl. I kissed her damp brow and hugged her and we sank into the cushions. I turned the lights off and held her in the darkness.

Emma

'Wowee!' Suki clapped her hands. 'Then what? Keep going!'

I sat up on the lounger, took a sip of my champagne. 'I fell asleep.'

Suki's eyes went wide. 'You fell asleep? No way!'

I nodded. 'It was bliss.'

'And you only have one fuck?' Suki looked incredulous.

'Are you kidding me? I felt . . . I felt like I'd being turned inside out and sent to heaven, Suki. No way could I have handled another.'

Suki grinned. 'He very good.'

'Good? He's amazing. The whole experience was amazing. Being shackled and blindfolded and pulled along past groping hands and probing fingers. And when . . .' Suki was rapt, licking her lips.

'When what? Please don't stop.'

When I sucked Sammy's tits, I was going to say. My God, what an experience. 'When tongues arrived, you know, below,' I said instead. 'By the time I entered the round room I was desperate for him.'

'And then you squirted!' she said excitedly and her words echoed around the spa. She clapped her hands again.

God yes, what the heck was that all about? 'Amazing,' I said. 'Jonathon Gold is truly amazing.'

Suki giggled and lowered her voice to a whisper, 'Mr Gold suits Emma Jane.'

I understood what she meant. He made me feel good. All that touching from strange hands, strange mouths, was just the build up to something magnificent – him. We fit together well.

Suki's eyes had gone to the ceiling. She was daydreaming about something. She sighed, picked up the champagne bottle and refilled our glasses.

'Is something wrong?'

She sipped her champagne. 'Oh no, Miss Emma.' She closed her eyes and breathed deeply. 'I just so happy for you.'

'Happy why?'

'Because you happy.'

She was right. I felt strong, confident. Empowered you might say. 'Tomorrow, what happens tomorrow?' Suki seemed to shrink at my question, seemed a little . . . afraid. 'Is it amazing? Is it wonderful? Is it . . . dirty?'

Suki shrugged, took a drink of her champagne. 'I don't know. Mr Gold didn't say.'

She was lying. I could read her like a book. 'He must have something planned, must have said something.'

'Well,' she put her glass down. 'He did suggest I should give you special Japanese massage. Suki do it very well.'

A massage did sound like a good idea. 'Yes,' I said. 'I'd like your special massage very much.' I glanced around the spa expecting to see a massage table I'd not noticed before.

'No, no, Miss Emma. Special massage tomorrow. Mr Gold wants to watch.'

My stomach tightened. Images in my mind. Suki caressing. Jonathon staring. But then . . . what? 'What makes this massage so special?' I asked.

Suki was shaking her head. Her cheeks were turning red. 'Suki say too much,' she said and ran a cutthroat finger across her neck. She got to her feet and took off her robe. 'Let's swim,' she said and with a flash of golden bikini she leapt into the pool.

I smiled after her, knocked back the rest of champagne. I was so looking forward to tomorrow.

Jonathon

Six

It didn't take long to find Emma. Although surnames are never used, I remembered seeing a photo of Fiona in the local rag and it had given *Bruce* as her surname. A quick Google search for Fiona Bruce brought up a charity article. The photograph showed Fiona and by her side was Roz, the filthy bitch Fiona often brought with her. *Roz Winters* the caption said – *sister of Fiona.* A quick image search for Roz Winters brought up an old photograph of horses with winner's rosettes. And there was a girl standing proudly with the winning horse. *Emma Jane – daughter of Roz.*

Emma Jane Winters – the name really suited her. I thought of her filthy mother, the things she liked to do. I had no doubt Emma Jane had any idea what her mother got up to, but I could now understand why Emma had taken so easily to the antics in the round room. She had *dirty* in her blood.

I drew a bath and sank into the hot water and the bubbles spilled over the rim of the tub. I relaxed back and closed my eyes and she was there, her face twisted in orgasm, then blissful release as her mouth opened wide and she let it all out, gushed all over my face and chest. She'd impressed me in the corridor; no resistance, no complaints, no hesitation, she'd went for it, full-on, and to fuck her afterwards, to be deep inside her as she came, as she'd screamed it out, was just so perfect.

As she'd drifted on an endorphin high I'd stroked her hair and breathed her in and thought of Heather. My Heather. They were similar but different. Emma was short, Heather was tall. Emma was a brunette, Heather a blonde. Emma had a young, chatty voice, Heather's was deeper, husky. But those were all physical differences. It was the spirit that was the same. Untamed, eager, a lover of life, a willingness to take it to the limits. But my Heather was gone.

I tore my mind away from painful memories and focused on the now. Emma Jane wanted to stay. Emma Jane wanted dirty. Well tomorrow I'd give Emma Jane Winters her money's worth.

Chapter Nine

The Dungeon

DAY THREE

Jonathon

'Yes, that's what I said, two roses, one white, one black, and make sure you check for thorns. Thank you, Annabelle.' I hung up the phone and rang Suki's room. She picked up with a groggy hello.

'Suki, it's early, I'm sorry, but I need . . . I need you.'

'Yes, Mr Gold. Where are you?'

'The dungeon. Come as you are. Come now!'

'Yes, Mr Gold. I'll be right there.'

The dungeon wasn't really a dungeon but the old Great Hall with thick stone walls and shuttered windows; a huge room with great length, complete with a well-stocked bar and every filthy implement a BDSM freak could ever want. Unable to sleep after tossing and turning with images of Emma's dirty hypocrite of a mother running through my mind, and thinking of the many implications, I'd been here since stupid o'clock, pacing the boards, drinking whisky, and pacing the boards some more.

I wanted to thrash Emma Jane, wanted to fuck her every which way, and I wanted her to have fun doing it, but I also wanted to tell her what her own sweet hypocrite of a mother gets up to once a month. But what then? That's what I couldn't fathom out. Would she walk away disgusted? Or would she shrug it off? Or would she tell her hypocrite mother to stick the wedding up her arse, because that's what she should do. That's what I hoped she'd do.

I looked at the crystal glass tumbler in my fist and felt the anger. I could almost crush it. Or launch it into the old stone fireplace. Instead I refilled it, drank it down, and refilled it again.

I collected up the printouts from the couch: pictures of Emma Jane and her horses, winner's rosettes pinned to their bridles. Pictures of Roz Winters at various events; one of her posing with the Mayor and his wife, a few at the local golf club's Christmas party, and half a dozen featured both Emma and her mother, and sometimes her hugely obese father; a leering *fat cat* if ever I saw one. I noted that in each photograph Emma was always at the back, kept behind, out of the spotlight. She looked so passive. Submissive even.

The sound of the old oak doors creaking open made me look up. Suki came striding across the room with her trademark grin. She was wearing a pink *Hello Kitty* nightdress. I turned the printouts face down and got to my feet.

'Is everything all right, Mr Gold?'

Her nipples were poking through her nightdress; her eyes were eager. 'No, Suki. Everything isn't all right.' I knocked back my whisky, placed the glass on top of the printouts. One nod to her midriff and she knew to remove the nightdress. She pulled it off over her head, threw it to the couch and stood before me with her hands behind her back and her legs slightly parted.

I didn't ask Suki what she would like, or how she was, nor did I consider her mood or the fact I'd pulled her from her bed before dawn.

'The four-way pulley,' I said and her face lit up.

She went to the pulley control on the wall and brought it down from the ceiling. I followed her, primal urges bubbling beneath the surface. 'I'm going to hurt you, Suki, how does that make you feel?'

'Excited, sir,' she said, adopting the position next to the shackles. Ramrod straight, hands behind back, legs slightly parted. 'But what about Miss Emma?'

'Miss Emma can wait, Suki.' I fastened the shackles to her wrists. 'Miss Emma told me she wants to be hit, wants to feel pain, wants it all. And, after giving it considerable thought, I realised that would mean pushing her towards heavy play.'

'Wow,' Suki said, shuffling her legs wide as I attached the spreader bar to her ankles.

'Yes, wow indeed.'

'Oh,' she said with a tone of disappointment.

I selected a coil of thin white cord and proceeded to figure-of-eight Suki's breasts. 'What is it, Suki?'

'Will I still get to give Miss Emma special Suki massage? I really looking forward to that.'

'Of course you will, and you will make it *extra* special.' I looped the cord through the centre of her breasts and up around her neck and she winced when I tied it tight at the rear. 'How does that feel? Nice and tight?'

'Hurts good, sir,' she said. 'Real good,' in a dreamy voice.

Her white breasts were squashed at the base, the protruding flesh beginning to redden, nipples filling out in response. I sucked each one in turn; sucked them to fullness, and Suki mewled a little. 'Cane or crop?' I asked her.

She looked at me with big grateful eyes, then to the various implements hooked on the rack against the wall, then back to me. She ran her little pink tongue over her lips, her breaths coming quicker now. 'Cane, sir,' she said.

Emma

It was after nine and there was still no sign of Suki. So I showered, wrapped myself in a fluffy robe, made a mug of tea, and took it to the bed along with my phone. I sent Aunt Fee a text.

`You're a minx. I fucking love you. xx`

I took a sip of my tea and her reply pinged.

`You're very welcome, darling. I fucking love you too. xx`

I was grinning at the phone when another text arrived.

`Didn't I tell you he was amazing?`

`You did`, I text back. `How's Venice?`

`Partying hard, darling. It won't be the same without me. Ha-ha.`

A knock on the door and I was surprised not to see Suki. It was Angel Annabelle pushing a serving cart and flashing her winning smile. 'Good morning, Emma.'

'Hi. Where's Suki?'

She lifted a bed tray from under the cart, snapped its legs down and placed it over my legs. I shuffled back against the pillows and settled the tray before me. 'I'm not sure where Suki is. But Mr Gold sends breakfast, with his compliments, and says that you should take your time and that he will be calling for you soon.'

She loaded the tray with enough food to fill a hungry horse:

scrambled eggs with smoked salmon, cream-cheese, two chocolate croissants, half a dozen rashers of crispy bacon, three slices of toast, butter, and a pot of what looked like orange marmalade. She topped that lot off with a cafetiere of steaming coffee – which smelled delicious – a jug of orange juice, and a bowl of fruit cocktail covered in yoghurt. Finally, she placed an ice bucket on a stand by the bed, opened a bottle of champagne, poured some into a flute and placed it on the tray, before sitting the bottle into the ice bucket. She took a step back, surveyed the feast before me. 'Ah,' she said, 'one last thing.' She dipped under the serving cart and came back with two roses. One rose was white, and I swear the other was so dark red it was almost black. What a nice touch. She placed the two roses side by side on the tray, gave a satisfied nod then flashed me a smile.

'Is this for real?' I said. 'I'll never eat all this.'

'It's what Mr Gold ordered. And he said to fill up, that you have a heavy day ahead.'

I felt my cheeks flush at that and looked away. 'Okay. I'll do my best.'

'Enjoy,' she said and I watched her leave.

A heavy day? I wondered what that could mean, but didn't think too much into it because I knew it would be pointless; Jonathon Gold could have anything up his sleeve if the round room was anything to go by. With a warm feeling flowing through me, I picked up the flute and started with the pleasant fizz of champers on my tongue.

Jonathon

'Tell me!' I said, well aware of the growl in my voice.

'Again . . . sir,' Suki breathed, sweat running down her face.

I pushed the cane to the floor between her spread legs then swung it sharply upwards, connecting with her cunt in a wet smack. She cried out, lost her balance, but the shackles held her in position.

'Tell me!'

'Again, sir.'

This time from behind. I pushed the cane to the floor between her legs and swung it upwards. Suki screamed and swung a little, again losing her balance, the shackles keeping her upright, the spreader bar keeping her open for me.

'Tell me!'

'Again . . . please, hit me again, sir.'

I swung hard at her ass and hit her so hard I felt the hit smarting through me. Suki screamed and bucked and I kept on hitting her. Six in quick succession across her ass. Six in quick succession across her thighs. Six in quick succession across the backs of her calves. Six more on her ass and she screamed with every delicious hit.

I moved around to her front. She was panting, tears streaming from puffed up eyes, mouth hanging open so invitingly wide. I removed my tee shirt, threw it to the floor, then brought the cane to her nipples; a sharp whack downwards to the right nipple, then repeated, rapidly, the smack, smack, smack a delightful fucking sound.

Suki screamed some more. I moved to the other nipple and smacked it hard. Suki screamed again.

I took hold of the crank and lowered Suki until she was leaning forward, arms stretched behind, feet awkward in the spreader bar, her head at just the right height. I took a collar and chain from the wall.

'You are a perfect angel,' I said as I stood before her.

'Thank you, sir.' She lifted her head, smiled up at me, then opened her mouth wide. I fastened the collar round her neck and undid the button on my jeans, pulled the zipper down, and brought out my cock, thick in my hand. I slapped her face with it. She kept her mouth wide, her little tongue flicking for it. Suki was expert at deep-throating; I was glad of that right now.

I wrapped the chain around my fist, pulled her to me and edged my cock between her lips and she sucked me into position. I pulled back a little, tilted her head to open her throat up and slid into her until her face was pressed into my stomach, and I kept it there, growling at the clench of her, at the feel of her throat constricting against the end of my cock. She snorted, gagged a little, but still I held her there, pushing with my cock, pushing so hard I knew I would soon come. Another gag, another snort, wetness running down my thighs. I pulled away and watched her gasping for breath. 'Tell me!'

'More,' she wheezed. 'More, sir.'

I went to the crank on the wall and turned it, lifting the hoist and Suki returned to vertical and her feet left the floor. I pushed her marked breasts and walked away, leaving her swinging. It was my turn to choose and the choice came easy. A hard-edge paddle. Leather stitched over wood, and a firm handle for gripping. The cat gut stitches in the leather added to the sting and always left marks.

I walked back to her with my cock standing proud, her swinging coming to a stop.

'Again, sir,' she said so softly, tears streaking her young face.

I moved behind her and caught her ass just right. She bucked and swung and yelped and my cock twitched for release. My nostrils were flaring, primal desire pumping at my fist. I hit her again and heard the sting of the stitches. A sting so beautiful I hit her again in the same place, over and over.

Her flesh reverberated with every hit; her head went back as she swung forward with the impact; my veined arm swung before me as I hit her again and again. And I didn't let up. I was spitting with the force of each hit and Suki screamed the rafters down; her screams pulling more strength into my strokes and I hit her again, this time I misaimed as she swung back towards me and the paddle caught her square in the lower back and she yelled blue murder. I hit her again, lower this time, across the tops of her thighs, and again, rapidly, grunting with every connection, and I just couldn't stop. I was seeing red. My cock was hard as iron, my heart thumping with adrenaline. Muscles bulging with the urge to . . .

Suki was shouting something. Babbling something I couldn't quite make out. Urge to what? The urge to maim? To control? To have pleasure? I threw the flogger down and made to grab Suki by the hips. I was going to fuck her brains out.

That's when I saw the blood trickling down her legs.

That's also when I realised she wasn't babbling at all; she was uttering her safe word.

'Bananas . . . bananas . . . bananas . . .'

Emma

`He sent me roses xx`, I texted, and followed it up with a photograph of the roses and the champagne on ice, and another one of the sumptuous breakfast feast.

Ping.

> `I'm jealous, little Emms. You must be doing something right (or WRONG) to deserve such treats xx`

I put the phone down and started on the eggs and salmon, when the phone pinged again.

A photograph: white crumpled sheets and the bottom half of tanned hairy legs entwined with Aunt Fee's legs, her toenails painted her standard blue. And beneath the photo: `About to have MY breakfast xx`

The old devil. I was looking forward to meeting up with her at the end of the week. I tucked in to the eggs, with toast, enjoyed the coffee, and wondered what Jonathon would have in store for me. I'd asked for pain, asked to be hit. My stomach tightened at the thought.

Jonathon

To say I was stunned was the understatement of the century. I'd never lost control before. Never.

Suki was sitting across from me on the leather couch, nursing her sore thigh with an ice pack.

I'd already apologised a hundred times, but she said it was fine, wasn't too bad, an easy mistake to make when you get carried away. But that's just it; I shouldn't have got carried away. 'I'm so sorry,' I said again, although I got the impression she was more disappointed that I hadn't fucked her.

'I'm worried, Mr Gold,' she said.

I looked at her. Her tits were still bound. 'Let me help you with that.'

'No, no,' she wagged a finger. 'Time is late. Miss Emma still waiting.'

'I sent her a big breakfast.'

'And now you going to hit Miss Emma?'

'That was the plan.'

'Maybe best to change plan?'

Change the plan? My blood was still boiling, the upturned printouts sat between us with my whisky glass on top of them and my dick was twitching in my pants. I realised then what I really wanted; what this rage was all about. I wanted to mark Emma Jane – mark her as mine.

I shifted the whisky glass and picked up the printouts, handing the one showing Roz Winters to Suki.

She looked at it for a moment, then at me, 'Client Two? The dirty one?'

I nodded, handed her one of Roz Winters with her daughter.

Suki stared at it for a second then her mouth fell open. She looked at me quizzically.

I took a breath, pinched the bridge of my nose. 'Meet Emma Jane Winters – our filthy client's daughter.'

Suki stood up, staring at the printout in her hands. 'Holy shit!'

'Exactly that,' I said.

'Does Miss Emma know her mother comes here?'

'I very much doubt that, Suki.'

She looked again at the printout. 'So . . . what are you going to do?'

Emma

I burped, unashamedly loud. Lots of sex – lots of good, horny sex – certainly gives one a hearty appetite. That and the champers. I'd eaten too much, and drank half the bottle of champagne. I lifted the bed tray to the bottom of the bed and settled back into the pillows feeling warm and special, closed my eyes and allowed my imagination to bring Jonathon before me, his cheeky smile, those gorgeous dimples, that naughty sparkle in his eyes. Jonny Gold was fun. My Jonny. I would definitely become a regular client; Jonny's *Six*.

Christ, would I have the balls to visit at the same time as Aunt Fee, and he could spank us together? Maybe not. I felt the smile spreading across my face. Aunt Fee would probably insist, though.

In fact, thinking of becoming a regular client brought me some hope; I'd have something to look forward to once I was married to Mr Fuck-me-on-a-Friday. Aunt Fee knew what she was doing. Jonny Gold made me feel good, made me feel strong.

I imagined his hands on my breasts, his mouth on my throat, soft and warm, his lips touching to my mine, his solid arms pulling me gently into him. Then he'd say something, and tickle me, and we'd laugh and he'd roll on his back and I'd climb on top and ride him. I turned on my side, my hand slipping into my bathrobe. Today was going to be a good day.

The door flew open and Suki marched in carrying a pile of clothes. I shrieked when I saw the state of her and almost knocked the bed tray over as I scrambled from the bed. 'What the hell happened?'

She was naked, bruised, her thighs and breasts laced with cane marks – and her breasts were tied up and looked extremely sore. Her eyes were puffed red, and her cheeks streaked with dry tears.

'It's fine, Miss Emma. Mr Gold just warming up.'

Warming up? My legs turned to water. I sat back against the bed.

'I brought you these,' she said and handed me the clothes. 'Get dressed now, Miss Emma. Mr Gold waiting for you.'

'Did it hurt?'

Suki grinned, 'Hurt real good. But hurry, Miss Emma.'

The clothes she brought weren't really me: a plain white bra, white lace panties, a blue cotton blouse with long sleeves, and a straight black skirt that came to just above the knee. I looked like I was dressed for the office. The sexy secretary type, I guessed.

'Heels,' Suki said, 'Mr Gold say to wear heels.'

'Heels? I didn't bring any.' I don't really like heels; rarely wear them. 'I've brought wedge sandals; will they do?' I fetched them from the walk-in and showed Suki.

Suki nodded. Dear God, her poor tits looked awful. I insisted on one more glass of champagne to calm my nerves before leaving. Perhaps by now I shouldn't be crapping myself, but I was. Suki joined me. 'To dirty clients,' she said as we clinked glasses.

'Where are we going?' I asked as we hurried down the stairs.

'The dungeon, Miss Emma. Really cool place.'

In less than a minute we'd arrived at a pair of huge double doors; thick oak and studded. They looked very old.

Suki looked me up and down. 'Ready?'

I straightened my blouse, my skirt. 'I think so.'

The sight that greeted me as she pulled me inside took my breath away.

'Wait here,' Suki said and walked hurriedly away to the centre of the enormous room, where I could just see Jonathon's head and shoulders from the back. He was sitting on a black leather couch, and was either naked or topless. He and Suki were talking but I couldn't make out what they were saying.

This was one giant playground – benches, cages, framework platforms, rows of costumes on hangers, shelves of dildos and wands and God knows what else – various pulleys and swings hung from the ceiling, and the walls were racked with hundreds of whips, canes, floggers – and the smell, a heady mix of leather and rubber.

I wondered what they were discussing. Suki was nodding, and I could see her big smile. Whatever it was I knew it would be about me, about what he wanted to do to me, and just the thought of that brought my tits tingling. I couldn't wait to sit on his cock again.

Suki was coming back. She looked happy despite her *injuries*. Surely he wouldn't cane *me* like that?

She took my hand and led me to stand before Jonathon, then stepped to one side, hands behind her back, feet slightly apart. I followed suit and felt like a minion brought before the boss. He was sitting on the couch wearing only jeans and a dark smile. His legs were open, and so was the button on his jeans.

'Good morning, Emma. I trust you enjoyed your breakfast?'

'I did, thank you.'

'Good, then you will have the energy for some serious play. Would you like to know what today's mission is?'

His eyes carried a strange look. Threatening? Wicked? Lust? All of the above? 'Yes, sir. Please, sir.' *I remembered the sir – go me!* He smiled at that.

He nodded to Suki. She took my hand and led me to a metal framework with two sets of chains hanging from it. It looked similar to the children's swings in the park but instead of seats there were cuffs at the ends of the chains. She fastened my wrists into the cuffs then raised the chains and locked them into place once my hands were level with my head. Then she moved behind me, out of sight.

Jonathon came to stand before me. Just the sight of his muscular torso and the hint of his tatts behind his open jeans made me hot down there. I took a breath, told myself to calm it down. I didn't want to come too soon.

'Are you comfortable?'

'Yes, sir.'

Another smile. He walked slowly forward, watching me, then passed by my side, his fingers trailing over mine. I wanted him to hold them, but he didn't. Now he was behind me. His hands touched to my waist and I felt the heat of him.

'You look beautiful this morning, Emma Jane.'

So do you. 'Thank you, sir.'

His grip became firmer, squeezing at my waist. I sucked in my tummy as he pressed and I swear if he kept up the pressure his fingers would touch in the middle. 'Beautiful,' he repeated and slid his hands up to my breasts, squeezing them gently, coaxing my nipples through my bra and blouse. I moaned into it, eyes closing as his warm breath caressed my neck.

'Limits,' he said. 'everyone has them, but most never get the chance to discover them.' He flattened my breasts to my ribcage and pulled me into his chest. 'Does that make sense, Emma Jane?'

'It does, sir.'

'Pain has limits, that much is obvious, yes?'

'Yes, sir.'

'Can you imagine what else has limits?' Warm lips touched to my neck and the slightest nick of his teeth made me shiver. The hairs on my neck prickled.

'No, sir.'

'Filth, Emma Jane. Some people think filth is shagging with the light on. Some people like to go to work with butt plugs up their arses. Some people to drink piss. It takes all sorts. How filthy are you, Emma Jane?'

I could feel the wetness in my panties. Just listening to his voice turned me on. 'Probably not very,' I said without much thought.

He let go of my tits and ripped my blouse open. I yelped as buttons went flying. He took hold of my bra cups in his fingers and slowly lifted them until my tits fell free, hard nipples catching on the taut elastic of the bra. 'Lower your head,' he said and his hands were now at my back, loosening the bra clasp.

I lowered my head. His hands returned to my front and he lifted the bra over my head and settled it behind my neck where it conveniently took most of the opened blouse with it. He loosened my skirt and it fell to my feet.

He came around to stand in front of me and stared at my breasts, my nipples dark and proud. *Suck them, please*, I wanted to say.

But he didn't do that. He came to me and tugged my panties down roughly. I stepped out of them and yelped when he smacked my pussy. He picked up my panties and brought them to his nose and inhaled. 'So sweet,' he said then smiled before getting down on his knees before me. 'Open.'

I opened my legs, my breathing heavy now. My face was burning, knowing his face was so close down there, but fuck this was horny. I flinched when he touched my pussy, a light stroking sensation on my lips, parting them with slow, delicate movements, exploring, searching; I leaned into it, enjoying the moan that escaped me.

Then something joined that probing finger, something rough, dry, and he was working it with his finger. I realised he was pushing my panties into me, all the way into me. 'Nearly there,' he said and gave a final push. He straightened up and gave my pussy a little tap. 'How does that feel?'

'Full . . . it feels full, sir.'

'Good girl,' he said. 'Your pussy looks quite stunning today.'

'Thank you . . . *sir*.'

'Have you ever pushed your panties up your cunt, Emma Jane?'

'Never, sir.'

'Good. Then you will enjoy the orgasm to come.'

He moved behind me, his warm hands clasped to my bare ribs. He squeezed at my flesh, massaged it, worked his way to my armpits, working his fingers into the smoothness, and I was so glad I'd remembered to shave them in the shower. His lips touched to my neck, kissed me once, twice, and again up to my ear. 'Pain,' he whispered and brought his hands to my breasts, nipples between thumbs and forefingers, rolling them, stroking them tight.

'Pain,' he repeated then grabbed at my breasts, squeezing hard and fuck it hurt. I stifled a cry, closed my eyes to it. He let go, then squeezed again, pulling me into him.

'Tell me you like it,' he said. 'Tell me you'd like your tits punished.'

'I like it, sir,' I gasped. 'Please punish my tits.'

'Louder!'

'Please punish my tits, sir!'

He squeezed again, so hard, twisting them away from each other. Shit, the pain, it was all I could do not to cry out. Then he let go again and my tits were red and aching.

'Suck them,' I breathed, 'please suck my tits, sir.'

He returned to my front, lifted my chin with a finger. 'Not yet. Suki, fetch the cane.'

Suki ran into my line of sight from behind, disappeared to the couch where Jonathon had been sitting, and came running back with a thin cane. To see her again, naked and with her breasts still tied and reddened, and the stripes and welts on her back, her ass, her thighs, made my heartrate go boom. I was going to get the same treatment. She flashed me a smile as she disappeared behind me.

Jonathon stood to one side and placed the end of the cane on my right breast. He gave a slight tap and I yelped. Fuck.

'It hurts,' he said. 'Even the lightest of strokes, especially when you're not used to it. Brace yourself.'

He brought the cane down, swifter this time, across both breasts; a hot slice of tender pain and I shrieked and jumped from foot to foot.

'Be still,' he said and hit me again. 'Tell me you want it.'

'I want it,' I gasped.

'*I want my tits caned*. Tell me!'

'I want my tits caned, sir.' Whack!

'*Cane my fucking tits*, ask me, Emma Jane, ask me!'

'Cane my tits, sir. Please cane my fucking tits.'

He whacked the cane downwards over both nipples and the pain was terrific. I clutched at the chains and swung a little and my right foot buckled as my wedge sandal gave way and came off. I hopped a bit before kicking the other one off and now I was on my toes.

'More! Ask for more!'

'More, sir. Please cane my tits, sir.'

I held on tight and gritted my teeth, determined to keep my eyes open, watching him.

He caught my gaze and paused. I saw the faintest flinch in his eyes, a blink, then it was gone. He focused on the cane, positioned it over my left breast, then he took a breath, steeled himself, and I watched him as he unleashed a torrent of smacks and by fucking Christ I screamed.

I panted, gasped, swung a little as I caught myself and he moved the cane to my right breast and hit me again, repeatedly, and I screamed it hurt so bad.

'I'm impressed,' he said. 'Feel that pain smarting, Emma. Feel it. Enjoy the ride as it throbs inside you, as it begs for salvation. Can you feel it?'

'Yes . . . I feel it, sir.'

'Good girl,' he said and held out hand. Suki passed him a coil of white rope and the man was quick, looping rope here and there so fast I couldn't keep up. With a final loop around my neck and a tightening tug at my back, my tender tits were bulging red from their bonds, the stripes where the cane had caught were darkening, blood pooling beneath.

'Perhaps now would be a good time to suck those beautiful nipples?'

'Please, sir,' I heard myself say.

His lips came to my left nipple and sucked it in and I swear I could feel the pleasure pushing its way through the pain. Now the other nipple, sucked right into his warm mouth and again the pleasure mixing with pain was something new, something amazing. My head went back and the shackles took some of my weight as he alternated from one to the other, sucking each nipple in hard then letting it go with a smack. Then he moved away, and I hung there, riding the thrill.

'How do you feel?' His voice cut through the haze.

'Horny, sir. So horny. Thank you, sir.'

'Hard pain and dirty pleasure, a potent mix, Emma Jane. Let's see how high we can go.'

His footfalls moving away brought me back to the present. He returned with a cheval mirror, one of those swivel oval ones on wheels – it looked almost the same as the one in my bedroom at home.

He positioned it in front of me. 'See how beautiful you look,' he said.

I looked a sweaty mess, all red and marked, breasts glistening with his saliva.

Suki arrived with a small crate. She placed it next to my left leg, lifted my foot, slid the crate under, and placed my foot on top of it. The image in the mirror made my clit pulse. The smallest piece of white lace was sticking from my pussy lips.

'I want you to watch,' he said, 'I want you to feel the sensations, yes?'

'Yes, sir.'

He nodded to Suki and she got down on her knees in front of me. In the mirror I watched as she edged her mouth closer to my pussy. She breathed on it and the tickle of her breath made my clit sing. I realised what she was going to do and once again my heart was booming.

Her lips touched to my pussy lips and her tongue flicked lightly over them sending a fluttering sensation through me that made me jerk away from her. She pushed a hand through my legs and clamped hold of my ass, and I watched again as she worked her little lips on mine, edging her face into me, parting my lips until her teeth found the jutting piece of my panties. There came a little tug and sparks flew, another tug as she slowly pulled away from me, the panties unfurling before my eyes. My clit throbbed and my pussy ached with pleasure as the lace material came away from me in short little tugs. The sensation was incredible.

Suki stood up and faced me with my panties hanging from her smile.

'Tell me how you feel now, Emma,' Jonathon said with a hand on Suki's shoulder.

'Horny, sir. I really need to come.'

He stepped up to me, undid my shackles and I fell against his chest. He held me there, stroking my hair. He left a kiss there, 'Beautiful,' he said and I believed him. This *was* beautiful, this moment, this time with him, and with Suki, discovering new highs, and I loved it.

He kissed my hair again then pulled away and brought Suki forward by the hand. 'Hug,' he said. 'Embrace each other.'

Suki made the first move, slipping her arms through mine and falling into me. Our bound tits touched and she squashed into me as I hugged her back. This was non-stop horny.

'Hold tight,' Jonathon said and there was a whack and a yelp from Suki as she jerked against me. Then it was my turn as he switched sides and the cane sizzled across my ass. Like stuttering puppets, we held tight and yelped and danced as he struck us over and over. My fucking ass was on fire, my tits were mashing sparks through me, and my pussy was begging to be filled. I prayed it would happen soon and yelped again as my ass stung.

Jonathon

I signalled a break, and, as prearranged, Suki opened champagne. I sat the two of them side by side on the couch, their tits still bound and marked. Emma Jane looked alive, awakened, and my dick twitched for her. But it would have to wait, because waiting made it greater. When I did come, the lovely Emma Jane would take the full force. I knocked back my champagne, it was time to push the dirty.

I pulled up a crate in front of the couch and sat facing the pair of them. Suki's eyes sparkled; she knew what was coming next.

'Emma Jane, you are almost halfway through your experience. And I'm so pleased with how you have handled yourself.'

'Thanks,' she said. Suki nudged her. 'Sir,' she added.

'What turned you on the most?'

She looked past me, thinking, then her eyes caught mine. ‘Everything, sir. I like it all.’

‘That’s not what I’m asking. I quite imagine you might *like* it all, but what was the horniest thing, the dirtiest?’

She looked past me again. ‘God, really, I don’t know. The strangers, in the round room, touching me intimately, that was super horny.’

‘Anything else?’ Her cheeks were as red as her bound tits. ‘Well?’

‘You shaving me, sir.’

I nodded.

‘And Suki, you know, touching me.’

‘Yes,’ I nodded again. ‘And?’

She looked blank.

‘How about when I swallowed your piss?’

She gasped at that.

‘In the round room,’ I went on, ‘when I sat beneath you on the bed and frigged your sweet cunt until you pissed on me.’ Another gasp, her look incredulous. ‘When you *squirted*,’ I emphasised.

‘I came, sir, I didn’t, you know . . .’

‘You came, yes, you experienced a bone-shaking orgasm, Emma Jane, but your squirt was not come. Rapid stimulation of the G-spot on the inside combined with carefully timed friction stimulation of the urethral orifice on the outside invokes an orgasm like no other and encourages the bladder to empty at the same time and with some eruptive force behind it. Your squirt was a mixture of piss and secretions from the paraurethral glands, Emma Jane.’

‘I see.’ She looked shocked.

‘Now that you know that, would you do it again?’

‘Yes,’ she said without hesitation.

'Good,' I said with a smile, 'then perhaps I will teach you how to execute the perfect squirt so that you might give the pleasure to someone else.'

'Yes, sir,' she said, again without hesitation.

'Do you think you have been dirty today, Emma?'

She drank her champagne. 'All this is new to me, so yes, every bit of it, I suppose.'

I sighed at her beautiful innocence, and took some moments to think about my next words. I had to get this right. I felt a little bad, really, maybe even guilty, but it had to be done. 'The limits of a person's dirtiness,' I began, 'are usually related to a person's upbringing and the environment of their formative years. Those limits can change, of course, when new experiences come along. I always take careful note of my clients' limits, after all it would be a useless host who did not adhere to his clients' needs.' Shit, she was drinking her champagne, losing interest.

'I have one client – we'll call her client number two – who loves piss, Emma Jane. She likes to give and receive. She likes to shove her pinkie down the slit in my cock, and she loves nothing more than rubbing her clit to orgasm while *my* pinkie is sunk knuckle-deep into her piss hole. It takes all sorts, ay?'

Now I had her attention. But she didn't say anything. I could tell she was a little embarrassed.

'Ever had a pinkie in your piss hole, Emma Jane?'

'No, sir.'

'Hmm.' I stood up and she stiffened her back. 'How are your tits feeling?'

'Numb, sir, and aching, and tender.'

'Good. And your ass?'

'Hot, sir, really hot.'

'Stand up.'

She finished her champagne, handed her flute to Suki and stood up. I passed my glass also to Suki and pulled Emma to me by the rope around her breasts. I reached around her to undo the slipknot, her hot breasts warmed my skin. I almost changed the plan, almost pushed her to the couch. I wanted her, wanted to mark her, but no, not yet.

Suki shifted the empty glasses to the bar and returned with our special toy in her hands. I watched Emma's reaction to it as I undid Suki's bonds. A reaction that portrayed both fear and desire; a perfect combination.

The *Starfish*, as Suki liked to call it, was formed from durable black latex with fine leather strapping. The black latex was a double dildo, complete with clitoral stimulator and a smaller urethra stimulator on the receiving end. Suki opened her legs and slipped one end of the dildo inside her while I fastened the strapping through her ass cheeks and around her waist.

'You look lovely,' I said to Suki and she gave me a little bow. Then to Emma, I said, 'You will enjoy this, Emma Jane.' She made to speak but Suki took her hand and placed it on the dildo jutting from her crotch.

'On your knees, Miss Emma.'

To my delight, Emma sank to her knees.

'Suck me,' Suki said and Emma Jane Winters opened her pretty mouth around that rubber cock and sucked it in. Oh how my dick responded as Suki moved slowly back and forth. Emma responded too; she brought her hands to Suki's ass and went with the rhythm.

'So good, Miss Emma, so, so good.' Suki withdrew, helped Emma to her feet and took a few short paces to a padded bench. She helped

Emma onto it and settled her onto her back, then the massaging began. Suki stood to the side of the bench, gently massaging, first Emma's breasts, then her stomach, thighs, and long slow movements back up again, spreading out across her shoulders. Emma closed her eyes, relaxed. I knew what she was feeling; Suki's little hands were quite magical.

Then she was climbing onto the bench, nudging Emma's legs apart, hands on her pussy now, rubbing, stroking. Emma moaned, moved her head to one side, hitched her legs a little in invitation and Suki took it, sinking the dildo into her.

The urge to release my cock was immense, the vision before me so erotic, but I held back, and watched as Suki fucked her, as Emma responded by lifting her legs around Suki's back and pulling her into her. Now Suki was moaning too, the pair of them writhing to the quickening beat. Suki was grunting, a rapid blur and Emma Jane was close, I could see it, the tells in her muscles tensing, contracting, relaxing, contracting, relaxing – soon she would burst. I moved closer to make sure I wouldn't miss the eruption.

At the first yelp and violent buck from Emma, Suki withdrew, grabbed hold of Emma's ankles and pulled her to the edge of the bench so that her legs hung to the floor. Suki dropped to her knees and thrust three fingers into Emma's engorged pussy and began to work it, rapidly in and out while catching her thumb on what by now would be a severely inflamed urethral opening. Emma would be feeling the sting, the burn of it.

Suki's thrusting fist turned into a blur and Emma Jane screamed, a beautiful sound and a beautiful sight as her body jerked and her arms flailed and her eyes caught the sight of her gushing over Suki's open-mouthed face. It was over in a heartbeat, but watching the comedown was divine. Suki gasping, her face and breasts dripping, a puddle around her knees on the floor. Emma, curling into herself, shuddering, taking great heaving breaths.

'I have high hopes for you, Emma Jane,' I said, when she'd caught her breath, 'client Six might yet become the dirtiest client of all. Sit up.' She did as she was told. 'Legs to the floor.' She touched her feet to the floor. I stepped up to her, close, and could not stop the urge to kiss her. I caught her face in my hands and pressed my lips to hers and she responded, kissing me back with passion. Her hands were at my jeans, pulling the zipper, my cock was in her hands and she did not stop kissing me as she pulled my cock to her pussy.

I lifted her leg and pushed myself into her. Her pussy was so hot, melting hot; she started to fuck me so I fucked her back and the kiss broke as her head went back. 'Oh God,' she said and I knew to withdraw because I was going to fucking explode.

'On your knees.'

She slid down my body and took my cock into her mouth, immediately gagging for taking it too far too quickly. I steadied her head with my hands and held her still as I fucked her, slowly at first, the tight grip of her mouth was torture. I pushed it further, just a little, and she opened for me and she held me there at the back of her throat for a good few seconds before she gagged again and pulled away, sending saliva down her front. I went in again, one last time. My balls were so tight, my cock so full. I pushed through her puffy lips and felt her tongue around my knob. I fucked her mouth again, sliding it in, this time with more of a thrust and she gagged but held and so I pushed again and my cock touched the wall of her throat and the first spasm arrived and I yanked myself out from her mouth and she took it full in the face, streams of cum up her nose, across her eyelashes and in her hair. I came long and hard, spasm after spasm until I was empty and my cum dripped off her chin. She looked up at me with a smile, scooped the cum up with her finger and sucked it into her mouth.

Emma

The water in the Jacuzzi was on high temperature, the bubbles set to a slow fizzle, the young woman sitting opposite me looked as happy as I felt.

'I think I'm in love,' I said and my stomach fluttered when I said it.

'Everyone love Mr Gold,' Suki said.

I knew he wasn't married or engaged. There were never rings on his fingers. Even if he took them off for safety reasons they would leave a mark, and there never any marks. 'Does he . . . does he have a girlfriend?'

Suki took a while to answer, and when she did she looked sad. 'No girlfriend.'

'Okay.' I felt I'd hit a nerve.

'Good play today,' she said, changing the subject but it was a subject I was happy to pursue. Strong images, and the strongest of them all was me on my knees and his thick white cum hitting my face. I could still taste it.

'Very good play,' I agreed. 'I'd do it all it again tomorrow.'

'Me too,' Suki grinned.

'What *is* happening tomorrow?' I asked, because I knew that Suki would know.

She shrugged. 'Mr Gold didn't say.'

Once again I didn't quite believe her. 'Did you know he sent me roses?'

Her eyes widened at that. She sat up. 'When? How? He did?'

'Yes, with my breakfast, two roses, one white, one black.'

Suki caught her breath. For a moment she looked horrified, then she tried to hide it. 'I enjoyed fucking you, Miss Emma,' she said, changing the subject again.

I smiled at the horny memory and my pussy tingled. I wanted to wear that thing next time, make Suki gush. I wanted to tell her that much but held back. 'I enjoyed it too,' I said.

'Really dirty. Dirty good for healthy mind, Miss Emma.'

'Speaking of dirty, what's she like?' I asked.

Suki looked at me quizzically.

'Client number two.'

Going by Suki's reaction, you'd think I might have told her I was about to kill her. She sat up with a strange look on her face. Embarrassment? Fear? Guilt? I'd obviously hit a sore spot.

She sank back into the water. 'Sorry,' she said.

'Do you not like client two?'

She looked at me with wary eyes. I wondered if she'd been abused or hurt by the dirty client. Maybe I shouldn't push it. 'It doesn't matter,' I said, 'I'm going to be the dirtiest client anyway.' I laughed, and Suki gave a weak smile. 'That was amazing what you did to me today. Thank you, Suki.'

She brightened a little at that. 'Miss Emma?'

'Yes?'

There was a long pause, as if she wanted to tell me something but couldn't – or wouldn't.

'Miss Emma, can I stay in your room tonight?'

Chapter Ten

Client Number Two

Emma

But we weren't to get straight to my room. As we exited the spa building and stepped into the warm evening air, still in our bikinis and wrapped in fluffy robes, Jonathon Gold was stalking across the lawns towards us. He'd changed into trousers, shirt and tie but looked a bit dishevelled, hair a bit crazy, and he was waving a clipboard about, grinning as he approached.

'Apologies for the impromptu interruption,' he said, eyes twinkling in the twilight, 'I've come up with an idea for tomorrow. Please, I need you both in my office.'

'Now, sir?' Suki asked.

'Oh yes. Right now.' He turned on his heel and marched off.

I looked at Suki. 'Is he . . . is he high on something?'

Suki looked suitably baffled. She shrugged.

In his office, he sat us down in those awful uncomfortable chairs before producing from the fridge a huge jug of iced lemonade and three glasses; one was a pint glass, the other two were tumblers. He filled the pint glass, passed it to Suki and told her *Demonstration shortly* to which Suki gave a little squeak, and by the time he'd filled the smaller tumblers and passed one to me, Suki's glass was empty. He filled it back up and she drank some more.

'Now,' he said, perched on his leather swivel chair, swinging a little from side to side. 'I thought, seeing as we are halfway through your experience, Emma, that we should take a pause to review and consider our options for the second half of your stay.'

'Okay,' I said. 'Makes sense.'

'On day one,' he was consulting his clipboard, 'I finger-fucked you on that very couch behind you.'

I glanced to the couch and back to him. Suki giggled.

'After that, I came to your room and shaved you before blindfolding you and fucking you in my arms.'

Shit yes. Tell it like it was, why don't you. My pussy quivered at the memory. He looked at me with a grin, his dimples seemed deeper than normal, his eyes darker.

'Day two,' he said, tapping the clipboard with a pen, 'was a sex feast. You earned a good spanking on the loveseat, before getting dirty with strangers in the round room. And then . . . and then you gushed for me and I fucked you until you screamed.'

I heard my own breaths, and my heartbeat. I glanced to Suki; she was gulping down more lemonade.

'And today, you experienced punishment and pain and the joys of a Suki massage.'

I was nodding at him, mouth agape, nipples puckering beneath my robe.

'You're a dirty, girl, Emma Jane.'

'Yes, sir. I am.'

'If you could pick one moment from the last three days, one moment that could almost bring you off just thinking about it, what would it be?'

That was easy. I looked him in the eye, burned my gaze into him and I saw the spark in his, the connection. 'Day one, sir, when you fucked me in your arms, when you picked me up and held me and slid me onto your lovely cock and I held my arms wide as you fucked me, and I felt like Kate Winslet on the fucking Titanic, God, Mr Gold, that was the best fuck I ever had.' *And I want you to fuck me like that forever.*

I took a sip of lemonade. It was getting really fucking hot in here.

'So, dirty girl,' he said, grinning, and I noticed the sheen of moisture on his brow. 'I suggest we explore your dirtiness. How does that sound?'

'That sounds good, sir.'

'Excellent. Then I'd like to begin by telling you something that my dirty client number two likes to do.'

Dirty client number two seemed to crop up every day. I wondered if he had a thing for her.

'Client number two has initiated many things here. But one thing in particular is particularly filthy. Imagine, if you would, client number two naked, on her back on a low coffee table and with her knees tied to her shoulders so that her pussy is on display.'

'Okay,' I said.

'Client two invites half a dozen of her kinky associates to attend what she refers to as her *dipping* parties. These men will fill her private places with mayonnaise and enjoy drinks whilst dipping with things such as sticks of carrot or cucumber.'

I couldn't believe what I was hearing. 'That sounds gross.'

Jonathon nodded, as if in agreement. 'It gets worse. By the end of the night each one of those men will have fucked her. Men who are mostly overweight drunks. And she loves it.'

The image in my mind of flabby men dipping their wicks into mush was not a pretty one. 'Yeah, definitely gross,' I said.

'Hmm,' Jonathon said, his eyes locked onto mine, elbows on the desk, hands clasped together. 'So you would not consider doing such a thing?'

Would I? 'Depends who's doing the dipping,' I said, and added, '*and* what the dip is,' and he smiled at that. 'I mean, that mayo must . . . *must* taste like crap, not to mention the smell. And the men are all flabby? Yeah, gross.'

'So you'd consider doing such a dirty thing, but you would be selective as to who could do the dipping. Is that what you're saying?'

I shrugged. 'I suppose.'

'Good,' he said and got to his feet, 'I have something to show you.'

Jonathon

I was pleased to get out of the office. It was far too warm in there. I allowed Suki to lead the way, wiping my brow while I was behind them, but my heart caught at what I saw. Suki linked into Emma, both in fluffy white robes. There was some whispering and giggling going on. I'd seen this image many times before. If Emma's hair had been blonde, this could have been Heather and Suki; the way they played and laughed together. I almost wanted to grab her by the shoulder and spin her around and kiss her and love her all over again. I wiped my brow again as we hit the stairs and forced my thoughts back to the task at hand.

We reached what was known as the golden room. I took a breath at the door. 'Before we go inside I must ask that you keep any chat to a whisper. We have a client in residence and must respect that.'

'A client?' Emma asked, suddenly looking a little afraid and again I wanted to hold her, kiss her gorgeous mouth.

'Yes,' I said, 'this is the golden room, an invention of client number two. Although client number two is not present, we do get other guests using the facility. So, quiet please.' I opened the door and we stepped inside.

Emma

The room was small and bright. White tiled walls and floor. And the drop in temperature gave me goosebumps. There was a golden chair with a plush purple seat that looked a bit like a throne. And the chair was facing a huge TV screen on the wall.

'Suki will demonstrate,' Jonathon said in a whisper.

Suki went to the chair and lifted the plush seat. It came up like a toilet lid and I noticed that's indeed what it was – a toilet bowl. Suki pushed her bikini bottoms to her knees, lifted her robe and sat down. At the same time the TV screen in front of her flickered to life.

On screen was a man, overweight and maybe in his fifties. He was strapped to a chair, wore a full head mask, and his belly hung so low I could barely see his dick.

'That's Barry,' Jonathon said in a whisper, 'a regular visitor to the golden room. If you haven't already guessed, Barry is sat directly beneath us. The toilet here feeds directly to a shower head positioned above Barry's head. When the seat is lifted the TV screen comes to life. Barry has a similar TV screen which comes to life at the same time. He gets to see who is supplying the shower.'

'Wow!' I said. *Client number two is one fucked up bitch,*' I nearly said but didn't.

'Suki, commence,' Jonathon said.

I heard Suki's pee whistling from her, pattering the toilet bowl, and on screen the flow was immediate. Barry's head was tilted back, mouth open, tongue flicking. I glanced to Suki who was leaning forward, elbows on knees, grinning at the TV screen, and back to Barry who was lapping it up. This was crazy, but kind of horny crazy. I found myself grinning too.

'So this was client number two's idea?' I said.

'Yes,' Jonathon said. 'It's rather dirty, isn't it? Is it something you would consider doing, Emma Jane?'

I didn't hesitate. As Suki returned to us and the TV screen went black, I marched right up there, lifted the seat, dropped my bikini bottoms to my knees and sat. The TV screen flickered to life and Barry looked at me. He cocked his head, blue eyes searched me through his mask, he smiled and I smiled back. Then I pissed and he tipped back his head and his pink tongue lapped it up. I glanced to Suki and Jonathon. Suki was silent-clapping and grinning like a loon. Jonathon was open-mothed – drooling if I wasn't mistaken. This was horny as hell. I felt naughty, dirty. I laughed out loud it was so crazy.

But Jonathon was waving me back and shoving me out into the corridor where Suki was giggling.

'I didn't mean for you to piss on the man, Emma Jane. I meant would you be on the receiving end.'

'Oh.' I shrugged. 'I think he enjoyed it anyway.' Jonathon was smiling. I think he enjoyed it too.

'You have spirit, Emma. I like that.'

'Thanks.' *You have spirit too. I like that.*

'Anyway,' he went on, 'as I was saying, the receiving end. Would you be there, under the shower head?'

Then a thought struck me. 'Is Barry there all the time?'

'Barry has been known to spend three weeks in the chair. Barry, not his real name, of course, is a VIP in the real world. His escape is here, where he spends days on end in the chair. And while he is in residence the angels use the golden room to pee.'

'All the angels?'

'Yes, all, male and female. Barry's not fussy and neither is your . . .'

'My?'

'Sorry,' Jonathon said, wiping his brow. 'Let me tell you what client number two likes to do. She'll throw a party in the spa for twenty or more angels. They drink, they fuck, they play, but one thing the angels aren't allowed to do is visit the toilet. Not until the party is over and client number two is strapped into the chair and one lucky angel, chosen by our filthy client, gets to kneel before her and eat her pussy while the angels above form a line.'

'My God,' I said.

'So, I ask you the same question, would you do that, Emma, be on the receiving end?'

I smiled at Suki and could almost read her mind. 'Yes,' I said, 'but again, I'd be selective.'

'Good,' he said, 'I'm pleased that you would be choosy, Emma Jane. I confess to seeing a great change in you in only three days. You have come out of your shell, and you are showing great spirit, not to mention enterprise. Tomorrow, then, shall be your day. *You* get to choose what we do. But the emphasis must be on exploring your dirtiness. I want us to discover just how dirty Emma Jane really is.'

My mind was whirring. My choice? In my mind I was dressed in leather and thrashing his ass with a flogger while he ate my pussy. That image was immediately replaced by his mouth, his lips on mine as he held me to him.

'We have everything imaginable here at your disposal,' he went on. 'Suki will fill you in and help with your selection.'

'Okay,' I said, heart beating madly at the thought.

'I suggest you breakfast in your room in the morning, and we'll reconvene in my office at 10 a.m. Oh, and you may dress as you please.'

'Sounds great,' I said, 'I already have some ideas.' *Though all I could think of were his lips on mine as he pumped me with his beautiful cock.*

'Good, then I'll wish you good night. And well done again, Emma. You're a changed person already.'

I thought about that, as I lay on my bed with my legs spread, waiting for Suki. The mood was right, of course. I *was* a changed person. Stronger, more assertive, maybe. Well, when it came to the sex bit, at least. I'd stepped up and pissed on Barry – no hesitation. And I'd found it horny as hell, Jonathon watching me, listening to me pee. The smile was still on my face right now, as Suki came bouncing back brandishing a razor and a small bowl of water. And she'd ditched the bikini. 'A quick shave to make sure you fresh for tomorrow,' she'd said. 'Really smooth for Mr Gold's tongue,' she'd said. Then she'd poked her own tongue out and waggled it.

It happened easily. It happened naturally. And now she was between my legs, making small strokes with the razor at the stubble. Then I heard the razor being dropped into the water bowl and her hand stroked my smoothness. 'All done,' she said and pressed a finger between my folds.

'Oh yes,' I said as she flicked her little tongue at my clit. I could feel the orgasm building within and I rode its warmth, its gentle push and pull.

She licked me up and down, slowly at first, catching my clit at every turn. Then came her little fingers, exploring, probing, and her thumb joined her tongue at my clit and the build-up turned into a burning thrum. My hands were squeezing at my tits, my ass writhing against her face, my breaths coming faster as she pushed and flicked and I was on the verge. A wet finger slid up my ass at the same time as she sucked my clit into her mouth and I came loudly, cursing and clawing at the covers and as the final pulse of pleasure hurled through me, she yanked that finger from my ass and it seemed to pull my clit along with it.

'Jesus,' I gasped, squirming away from her still-gobbling mouth.

She was grinning at me, her face dripping.

After showering, we lay on the bed in our robes, drank tea and talked.

First it was about Heather. 'She had fun spirit, like you,' Suki said. 'Mr Gold love her very much. So did Suki.'

I asked where this Heather was, what had happened to her, but didn't expect what Suki said next.

'She died, sixteen months ago. One day she had stomach pains, next day she was told she had lots of cancer inside. There was nothing the doctors could do. She died a week later.' Suki wiped tears from her eyes.

'And they were married?'

Suki shook her head. 'No. Heather said she didn't need a piece of paper to tell her who she loved.'

'Oh God,' I said, 'the poor woman. And Jonathon. Poor Jonathon.'

'Mr Gold sad for long time. But Miss Heather made him promise to keep the business going.'

'I see. And what about this client number two – does he love her? Is that why he's so obsessed about her?'

Suki gasped at that. 'Oh no, Miss Emma. No love at all.'

'Then why does he keep bringing her up?'

There was a pause as Suki stared into her tea and considered this. 'Well,' she said, 'I think it's because he likes you.'

'That doesn't make sense.' *I like him too.*

'Yes it does, Miss Emma. You see, client two is really filthy and doesn't care whose dick she takes or who pees on her. But when Mr Gold ask Miss Emma, you say no, you would be choosy. That's what Heather would have said. Mr Gold likes that. Likes you.'

I heard what she was saying, and could see where she was coming from but couldn't quite believe it. There was more to it than that. The man seemed obsessed with client number two. I decided to push Suki a little. 'Client number two . . . what's her name?'

Suki blushed at that. She actually blushed. 'More tea?' she said but I stopped her from getting off the bed.

'There's something you're not telling me, Suki.' Now she looked scared, bless her. 'You can tell me. Whatever it is can't be that bad, can it?'

She shook her head. 'Sorry, Miss Emma, I'm not allowed to say anything about other clients. Doing so can get me fired.'

'Jonathon wouldn't fire you. Trust me on that, Suki. You're just too damn nice.'

She smiled. 'Thank you, but I must respect rules.'

I took her hand in mine. 'I promise not to say a word outside of this room.'

Silence.

'Suki, whatever it is can't be that bad. And even if Jonathon fired you, I'd hire you in a heartbeat.'

'You would?'

'Absolutely. On the spot. You could be my PA for life. In fact, I might just steal you from Mr Gold anyway.' She laughed at that. 'Please tell me, Suki.' She blew out a breath, licked her lips, looked nervous. 'Please? It'll be okay, I promise.'

'And you promise not say anything?'

'Yes, I promise.' I squeezed her hand.

She took another breath and I felt my heart thudding in anticipation.

'Client number two . . .'

'Yes.'

'She visits at the same time as your friend.'

'My aunt? Aunt Fee?'

Suki nodded.

'Do I know her?'

She nodded again. 'I think so.'

Then I imagined Aunt Fee with her knees roped to her shoulders and being filled with mayo and dipped – and then in Barry's seat, and a line of angels above. 'Good God, Aunt Fee, does she –'

'No, no, Miss Emma, your aunt not so filthy, she only likes pussy pamper, and she likes Mr Gold fuck.'

Images of Suki licking Aunt Fee, and Aunt Fee slotted onto Jonathon's cock while she hung off of him Kate Winslet-style were weird enough, and I felt a pang of jealousy, but still I was relieved she wasn't into the really filthy stuff. I took a breath, 'Good, so, filthy client number two – what's her name?'

Suki turned her eyes down, away from mine.

'She has a name, right? Suki?'

I swear I heard her swallow. She looked up. 'Yes, she does . . .'

I nodded. 'Go on.'

'Client number two is known as . . .' Now her cheeks were beetroot. I held my breath. '. . . client number two is known as . . . Miss Roz.'

It only took a second for the penny to drop. Client number two was my own fucking mother. I hadn't been able to speak at first. And it seemed neither could Suki as she followed me around with a hand over her mouth as I packed my case. I couldn't believe it. And the audacity of the man.

I was almost in tears as I slipped my engagement ring back on my finger.

'Miss Emma?'

'He fucked my mother, Suki. My own mother. In fact, scratch that, he *fucks* my mother. Because she'll be back and he'll do it again, just for dirty client number fucking two.'

'Please, Miss Emma, it's not like that. Please stay.'

'Of course it's like that. He fucks my mother, and he *knows* he fucks my mother, so why wouldn't he tell me? He should have told me, Suki.'

'But it's not Mr Gold's fault. Please give him a chance.'

I looked at Suki. She was crying. 'I'm sorry, Suki. I can't stay here.'

Chapter Eleven

No Socks

DAY FOUR

Jonathon

Last night was a washout. After leaving Emma and Suki I'd hit the shower and relived her; the smell of her fresh from the spa, her newfound brazenness, and the way she'd stepped right up and pissed on Barry without the slightest hesitation. Emma Jane Winters was highly sexed and kinky, just like her mother, but there was a subtle difference. Emma Jane cared.

I'd thought about telling her who client number two was, and what the consequences might be. *I'm sorry, Emma Jane, but I've fucked your mother's every hole and in every which way. Your mother likes to serve food from her snatch, the messier the better, and she invites just anyone to dip their flabby wicks. Your mother loves piss so much I firmly believe if she could choose her own death she would like to drown in it.*

I imagined Emma's head exploding. That she'd go crazy, and march right out of here in an instant and I'd never see her again. Client confidentiality was obviously the way to go.

Now I was in my office, at the PC, searching for websites of churches in the area.

St Mary's website showed the marriage banns for three couples. But no Emma Jane.

St Peter's listed eleven upcoming marriages – no Emma Jane.

St Mark's website was bright yellow and garish, a huge advert for roof-fund donations took up most of the front page. I clicked on *marriage banns* and there were only two listed. Emma's name jumped out at me.

BANNS OF MARRIAGE BETWEEN

William Ruben Ripley – *of this parish*

And

Emma Jane Winters – *of this parish*

Bingo! I wrote down Ripley's full name. Now I needed the father. He was simple to find. A search for images of Roz Winters brought up three with him in the frame. An obese and lecherous-looking man. Arnold Winters the name.

I had my names. It was time to do some digging, contact some friends in the trade and see if I could find anything on them. But when I opened up email I was surprised to see one there from Fiona, the subject heading: *Checking in.*

I opened the mail.

> *How's my friend? Is she doing all right?*
>
> *Fx*

I fired one straight back:

> *Your NIECE is doing really well.*
>
> *Jx*

The reply was immediate,

> *My niece? You know? What else do you know? Oh,*

can we text? It'll be so much easier? Here's my number, 555 2671460

So I picked up my phone and texted,

`I know that I fucked her dirty mother.`

She texted right back,

`Yes, the filthy cow. But Emma Jane and you, I knew you'd like her. I knew you'd make a great couple!`

`Couple?` I texted back.

I waited for her reply for what must have been a full minute before my phone pinged.

`Oh screw this. I need to speak to you. It's important. Give me five minutes to get the serving boy from my room and I'll ring you. Yes?`

I confirmed with a `Yes` and poured myself a coffee while I waited. I had a feeling some great revelation was on the horizon but for the life of me I couldn't imagine what that might be.

Ten minutes later my phone rang.

'You said five minutes.'

She laughed. 'Anticipation, Jonathon.'

I gave a polite laugh at her joke. 'So, what is it that's so important?'

'Get a pen and a pad, Jonathon.'

'Right here,' I said pulling pen and pad towards me.

'Write down these names . . .'

She gave me the two names I'd just searched for myself. 'That's funny,' I said, 'those names are already on my pad.'

A pause. 'Why?'

'I . . .' I realised I should have perhaps kept that to myself.

'Jonathon? Were you doing some digging? You were, oh you were, weren't you?'

I sighed. 'Maybe I was,' I said. 'I'm just a bit concerned about, you know, Emma.'

'The wedding, you mean?'

'Yes, that.'

'Concerned or in love?'

'What?'

'You heard me.'

'Concerned, like I said.'

'She's marrying a bastard.'

'I thought as much.'

'And her father's a hideous cunt.'

'Strong words. I felt the venom in that.'

'You bet.'

'And you've given me their names because?'

'I want you to do some digging, Jonathon. And I can show you where to dig.'

'Go on.'

'You are on friendly terms with the proprietors of establishments similar to your own?'

'Of course, with pretty much most of them. We share blacklisted clients, risky clients, that kind of thing.'

'I thought as much. Write this down . . .'

I wrote down what she said.

Club Explicit – in the city, Arnold Winters – blacklisted.

Club Berry Berry – Herefordshire – William Ripley

enjoys Thursday evenings with his Ginger Berry club mates fucking his favourite Filipino nineteen-year-old.

'You're kidding me?'

'No, I am not. Emma's parents and that awful Ripley are pushing her into a marriage purely for the means of making money. But they're despicable hypocrites, Jonathon. I promise you, contact your friends, and when you find out what I know, you will see that Emma does not deserve this.'

'What *you* know? Why not just tell me?'

'You need it from the horse's mouth, so to speak. You need evidence. Listen, Jonathon, Emma Jane, she . . . she deserves better. And you, you have the means.'

'Right,' I said, 'but what makes you think I want to go digging up the dirty on these people? It's hardly my place to –'

'Jonathon, you were going to dig anyway.'

'Ah, yes, well. All right,' I said, 'Thank you, you might have saved me a lot of work.'

'You're welcome, Jonathon. And remember, *you* have the means.'

I glanced at the clock on the PC – ten minutes to ten – Emma and Suki would be here soon. Just enough time to fire off two emails.

I knew Andy at Club Explicit well. We went back to college days and often helped each other out. As Fiona had suggested, I asked him for any information on Emma's father, Arnold Winters.

Jessica Jones at Club Berry Berry might not be so helpful. She supplied the punters for Roz Winters' dipping parties, so I would have to tread carefully. I gave her the name William Ruben Ripley and asked very nicely for any information. I sent the email and shut down the PC.

Emma

Suki slept in my bed last night. She persuaded me not to do anything rash, to at least sleep on it. And I couldn't leave her sobbing, so I agreed that I would wait until morning before leaving. But I found myself being swayed. Suki talked more of Heather, of how kind and loving she was, of how strong she was. Of how she could fuck twenty angels in one session and keep on going like a Duracell bunny. Miss Heather was cool. Miss Heather had built the secret garden, the loveseat, and the roses of pure white and those that she'd bred and nurtured to be so deep red they were close to black, were symbols of her and Jonathon. He kept her darkness at bay with his brightness, his cheeky smile. I could see that, could feel it, and like a fluttering moth to a hot-as-fuck flame I was liking Jonathon Gold all the more – despite the fact he'd fucked my mother.

Suki urged me to stay and reminded me that today was my choice. I could do whatever I wanted to do. So we bandied some ideas about, and they were good ideas. I'd need a car and Suki's Suzuki jeep would be perfect. The blonde wig from the props room made me look a bit like Uma Thurman, and Suki's big sunglasses finished the look. It was a suitable disguise for going out and about.

Jonathon.

Ten on the dot, the knock on the door came.

Suki came breezing in as if she was ushering in a princess, and maybe she was. Emma Jane took my breath away. She wore a summery yellow dress that came to just above her knees and she looked truly radiant. I noticed she had a bag over her shoulder, and that she wasn't wearing a bra.

I motioned them to the seats in front of my desk and sat myself down.

'You slept well?' I asked.

'Yes, very well,' Emma said, and she and Suki smirked at each other.

'And you've decided what you'd like to do today?'

'I have,' she said. She rummaged in her bag, pulled out a compact mirror and applied some cherry red lipstick, pursing her lips at me. She next pulled out a blonde wig I recognised from the props room. She finished the look with Suki's big round sunglasses and blew me a kiss.

'Very nice,' I said, quite amused. She looked beautiful, and . . . *happy*. I found myself smiling back at her. She went back in her bag and pulled out a set of keys. Suki's car keys. I knew the Miss Kitty keyring.

'We're going to have some fun in the sun,' she said, jangling the keys in the air. She got to her feet. 'I want you out front in ten minutes. And don't wear any socks.'

'No socks?' I raised an eyebrow.

Chapter Twelve

Playing footsie

Emma

Jonathon had opted for stonewashed cut-off jeans and a pale blue cotton shirt, sleeves turned back, neck open down to his chest. Despite the bump and rattle of Suki's jeep and the *Miss Kitty* air freshener and the *Miss Kitty* steering wheel cover, the *Miss Kitty* stickers all over the dashboard and the *Miss Kitty* fluffy toy hanging from the rearview mirror, the air in the cab felt supercharged. His combo showed off his tanned calves and toned chest. He looked fucking hot. Oh, and deck shoes, easy to slip off and on – and no socks as I'd requested, and now I was getting hot, sweaty. *Nervous.*

'Penny for them?'

I actually gasped as his voice broke my thoughts. I glanced at him, flashed him a smile. 'Sorry . . . I was miles away.' Eyes back on the road, I gasped again as a baby rabbit appeared from nowhere and vanished under the jeep as I went straight over it. I gripped the steering wheel and my heart was in my mouth, waiting for the bump.

But in the rearview mirror the baby rabbit was hopping away into the grass. 'Shit,' I breathed.

'Sorry,' he said, 'didn't mean to break your concentration.'

I rolled my window down a bit, glad of the breeze.

'The day's heating up already,' he said, rolled his window down too and cool air whipped around us.

'Yeah,' I said, 'it's going to be another scorcher . . .' I took a sweeping turn in the road and the jeep rattled over the first cattle grid. We were hitting the moors now.

'Where exactly are we going?' he asked.

I smiled at the thought. 'Somewhere . . . *weird*,' I said.

'Weird?' He laughed. 'I like weird.'

His words invoked an instant image of my mother sitting on his cock. I shivered and batted her from my mind. 'Not that kind of weird,' I said and thought about baby bunnies instead as we rattled over another cattle grid. I slowed the jeep as we approached an opening in the hedgerow and took us through it onto open field.

'Sex in the great outdoors,' he said, winding his window all the way down and resting his arm on it. 'I do like a good fuck in a field on a hot day.'

'You've got sex on the brain.' I took the jeep up a low hill and to a thick copse of trees, where the shade of overhanging branches would keep the jeep hidden from distant eyes. I killed the engine, took the binoculars Suki had found for me from my bag and focused on the stables. Tommy and Marcus were leading Gem and Siri to the paddock. And Graham the gardener was overseeing a feed delivery. All looked well, although I did have the urge to run down the hill and leap onto Gem's back. I was missing her. I imagined Jonathon down there with me by his side, brushing down the horses together, mucking out together, *riding on the moors . . .*

'That's your place, I guess?'

'Yeah. I couldn't resist a peek. I miss my horses. Do you ride?'

Apart from my mother. And she was back, screaming like a whore as Jonathon fucked her.

'No,' he said in a tone that felt distant, as if there was a *but* coming.

I pushed my mother away into darkness. 'But?'

A pause. 'No buts.'

I almost stopped myself, but the words came out, 'Heather, did she ride?'

He looked at me. 'Heather?'

'Suki told me about her. I'm so sorry.'

He looked away, took a breath. 'Heather had ideas. She rode in her youth, and wanted to get back into it. Said riding a horse well, depended more on the horse's trust in the rider than anything else. That if you loved the horse, the love was reciprocated like nothing you could imagine.'

I swear I felt my heart melt. 'That's so true.'

'When she first bought the old place, she did so because it already had the set-up; stables, tack room, paddock, although they hadn't been used for years. She wanted to do it all up, teach me what she knew. But it wasn't to be.'

'I'm sorry,' I said again. 'I didn't mean to . . .'

'So, to answer your question, the nearest I've been to a horse is I have vague memories of riding on a donkey on Blackpool beach when I was little. Anyway,' he sat up, turned to face me. 'Back to today. What's on the agenda?'

I could teach you, I wanted to say. 'I already told you, I'm taking you somewhere *weird*.'

I started the engine and took the jeep over the brow of the hill, hoping no one on the yard would think to follow.

Jonathon

After a bumpy ride we pulled up at an old stonewall sheep pen. 'This is it,' she said.

'This is the *weird*?'

She smiled at me from behind her big sunglasses. 'Come and see.' She stepped from the jeep and disappeared inside.

When I entered the pen the sight that greeted me caught my breath. The wig and sunglasses were on top of the wall by her side. The strong sunlight behind her enriched her auburn hair to a fiery red and at the same time it made her yellow dress almost see-through, the curves of her breasts and hips so prominent. She looked stunning.

'I did some figuring out,' she said as I approached her.

'Oh?'

'Yeah. Over the last ten years I've visited this old sheep pen many times. Although mostly I don't stay long. Just long enough for the chosen stable boy to get his inexperienced rocks off and for me to get a thrill.'

'I see. And I'm today's chosen one?'

'No, not today.' She ran her hands through her hair, pulling it off her brow. Her face glistened in the sun. I could feel the sweat on my own brow. This place was a little suntrap. 'I want to do something here I've never done before.'

'Which is?'

'Can you guess?'

'Why not just show me?'

To one side of the pen the stonewall was damaged, the wall was lower, and a flat slab of stone had been put on top to create a narrow seat. I guessed that Emma might have done that herself. She went to the seat and sat down and patted the space beside her.

Emma

There wasn't much room. When he settled beside me his bare arm touched to mine and my skin prickled softly. I slid my arm through his. 'I've never done this before.'

'This?'

'Shared this seat with anyone. My thinking seat.'

'So you come here alone sometimes?'

'Believe it or not, yes. I'm not a total nymphomaniac, you know. I come here to think.'

'What do you think about?'

'Actually that's not true,' I said and I saw that he was looking at me but I kept staring out over the fields. 'I come here to escape. To breathe in the freedom where I can just be me, with my horse, and only the insects telling me what to do. I like the peace. The quiet.'

'It's good to get away from it all now and then,' he said. 'Good to have a private place.'

'But you're here now,' I said, squeezing his arm to me. 'Sharing it with me. And . . .'

There was only the low drone of a distant airplane crossing the clear blue sky.

'And?'

'There's something else I've never done here before.' I turned my head to look at him and our eyes connected with a smouldering intensity that pulled us together. His full lips touched to mine and our eyes closed to the kiss, warm and slow, his hand in my hair, my hand in his, and the kiss went on, gentle and probing, and my heart beat for this lovely man.

We stopped for breath and he kissed my chin, my jaw, my neck, where he paused to suck a little before our lips were touching again. My hands held his face and we kept on kissing when he tugged me to my feet and slid his hands around my waist and pulled me to him. Slow, probing kisses under the heat of the sun and the only sound the buzz of a nearby bee. His hands travelled up my ribs, to just below my breasts and the urge to let go, to strip off, to make love right there was almost too much. I pulled away from him, caught my breath.

'Thank you,' I said. 'That was everything I imagined it would be.'

'That was it? Just a kiss?' His hair was damp, his face sweaty, and so was mine.

'Yes. Just a kiss.'

'Oh.'

'Oh?'

'I thought we might, you know.'

'I've done the *you know* here more times than I care to remember,' I said. 'But never a kiss, a real kiss with a real man.' *A heartfelt kiss. A loving kiss. A reciprocated kiss.* 'How was it for you?' *Because for me it was beautiful.*

'The kiss?'

'Of course the kiss.'

'Very nice.'

'Just very nice?'

'You taste good. I like the way you taste.'

That sparkle was in his eyes, the cheeky grin, the cute dimples. God I loved this guy. 'You taste good too,' I said and once again I was in his arms and our lips touched softly, warmly, his firm hands at my ribs, and I was aching for him. I could feel the tension between us, the need for naked release as his hands cupped my breasts. I knew that any more and my dress would be off. But I didn't want that. Not here. I pulled away, stroked damp hair from his brow. 'You hungry? I know a great place.'

Jonathon

'Ravenous,' I said, my cock pushing at my jeans. She picked up the wig and sunglasses and held out a hand. I took it and she led me back to the jeep. And so we drove on. And I was enjoying it, the day, the sunshine, spending time with a beautiful woman. I could taste her on my lips. Emma Jane had me; a siren reeling me in.

'Here we are,' she said, pulling into the Crab & Lobster's car park.

A waitress dressed in black with a white apron spotted us stepping inside and came straight up to Emma. Dark curly hair to her shoulders, pale-skinned and curvy hips. *Maria* her name badge said. My cock twitched at the thought of flogging her ass. Emma caught my eye and I looked away.

Maria led us outside to the corner of the busy beer garden, and a table set for two and with a Reserved sign and a bottle of champagne in a cooler.

'You okay with lamb shank?' Emma asked. 'It comes highly recommended.'

'Sounds good,' I said, catching the spark in Maria's eye. She smiled, said thanks, and that it wouldn't be long, before leaving me with a view of her shapely ass as she crossed the lawn.

'Jonny boy? Yoo-hoo!'

'Jonny boy?' I turned back to Emma.

'Feeling horny are we?'

'Just a bit.' I indicated the champagne. 'You rang ahead?'

'Of course. I promised the lovely Maria a generous tip.'

I popped the cork, filled the flutes, and we drank. She looked lovely in the blonde wig, so different. And with the lipstick and the sunglasses it could almost have been Heather sitting opposite.

'Take your shoes off, Jonny,' she said in a whisper.

I looked at her. My mother used to call me Jonny. I'm not sure it suited me now, though.

'Take them off, Jonny and make sure no one sees what you're doing.'

I drank my champagne, kicking my shoes off at the same time.

'Are they off?'

'Yes.'

'Touch me,' she said and moved forward on her seat.

Now I realised why she'd asked me not to wear any socks. My cocked pulsed its approval in my jeans.

I scanned the tables behind her. No one appeared to be paying us any attention. I carefully touched my toes to her leg, skin touching skin, and she gave a little flinch. Her calves, soft and warm as I felt my way up them. She tensed when I reached her inner thigh. Her breath hitched and we smiled at each other and drank our champagne. An almost imperceptible nod and I felt her legs parting, allowing me to take my toes forward and I was amazed that I could feel the heat of her before my toes connected with her wetness. She was slick, and soft, almost creamy as I ran my toes between her folds. 'More,' she gasped, 'that's so nice.' I stroked up and down and she exhaled deeply, her face flushed, her mouth hanging open, and I knew that behind the sunglasses her eyes were closed. 'Christ,' she whispered as my big toe found her clit, a hot little nub of pleasure. I circled it gently, watching the people around us enjoying their lunches in the sun, only the sounds of chatter and laughter and cutlery as Emma Jane's breathing stuttered. 'Don't stop,' she said.

If my cock had a tongue it would have groaned and licked itself. 'You're amazing,' I said.

'So are you,' she said and pulled away from my probing toes so they were resting against her pussy lips.

'You said not to stop?'

'I need a break. I'm close to coming,' she breathed. She dipped into her bag and pulled out her phone. 'Smile,' she said and took my photograph. 'For posterity. When I look at this I'll remember what you were doing.'

'Good idea,' I said, taking out my phone. 'Can I have one without the wig and glasses? No one is looking this way.'

She glanced around her, her cheeks flushed, her brow a fine sheen. 'All right. But be quick. Tell me when you're ready.'

I framed her lovely face. 'I'm ready.'

'Anyone looking this way?'

'No.'

She whipped off the wig and glasses, puckered her lips at me and I clicked the button. The wig and glasses were back on in a blink. With my toes still touching her, I showed her the picture.

'I look like a desperate bitch in heat,' she said.

I laughed at that, wriggled my toes against her soft pussy lips and reminded her that perhaps she was.

I spotted Maria coming through the far doors, carrying two plates. 'Here's our food,' I said and pulled my foot away.

'*No*,' she hissed. 'Put it back. Now! And keep it there while you talk to the nice waitress.'

'You serious?'

'Do it!'

I found her folds, pushed my toes a little deeper, and stroked upwards to her hard little clit and Emma stiffened and clamped her mouth shut. She picked up her champagne and gave me a strained smile as I flicked her clit with my big toe.

'So, that's all there is to it,' I said as Maria arrived, placing our plates of lamb shank on the table. 'We'll dip our toes in, see how it pans out. Yes?'

Emma nodded, mouth still clamped shut, breathing through her nose. She raised her glass to her lips and took a drink. I wriggled my toes and she coughed and spluttered her champagne.

'That looks delicious, thank you, Maria,' I said, pressing my toes against Emma's hot clit.

She clasped her knees shut, trapping my foot.

'Enjoy your meal,' Maria said and walked away.

'Bastard,' Emma said with a laugh. 'And take your eyes away from her arse.'

'But it's a nice arse. Perfect for flogging.'

'Will you stop that?' She released my trapped foot and pushed my leg away.

'Stop what?'

'Ogling. This is meant to be *our* day.'

'Sorry. It's in my blood, I think. Always on the lookout for potential angels.'

'What about me? Do I have angel potential?' She looked over her glasses at me and fluttered her eyelashes.

'Oh yes, Emma Jane, you would make an amazing angel.'

'Is that an offer?'

I laughed. Emma Jane was more than an angel. Emma Jane could be mine – a leader of angels. 'I'd love to have you around . . . permanently,' I said and my words hung in the air between us.

Emma

My stomach tightened at his words. A permanent angel? Or a permanent partner? I was too scared to take it any further.

'What's next?' he said, cutting into his lamb and taking a bite. 'You were right by the way, this is delicious.'

'Up to you,' I said. 'Do you fancy a dessert?'

He laughed and red-wine sauce dribbled over the corner of his mouth. He licked it away. 'Not what I meant. I meant what other surprises do you have up your sleeve?'

I gazed into his dreamy eyes. A permanent partner. Hand in hand. Walking the grounds. Tending the garden. Heather's roses. Making love on the loveseat. Spanking. Laughing. Doing up the stables. Riding horses. All of those things seemed to be up my sleeve, waiting to happen. Aching to happen. But dreams were dreams, weren't they? At least until something clicked and a dream could become reality.

'Are you all right?'

He was staring at me. And I held his gaze, breathed him in, soaked him in, ached for him. I was falling for Jonny Gold. I wanted his hand to take mine, wanted him to say he felt the same way. 'Sorry. Daydreaming,' I said.

'You seem to do a lot of that.'

'I like to dream. Gives me hope.' *Please take my hand.*

'Want to share?'

And there goes my thudding heart again. 'Dreams don't come true if you share them,' I said in a voice that came out shaky.

'I thought that was wishes?'

'Wishes?'

'Yes, my mother would always say that if you shared a wish it would never come true.'

'Dreams, wishes, same thing. So I'll keep them to myself, just in case.'

'All right, so answer my original question.'

'Which was?'

'What surprises do you have up your sleeve?'

'You're eager.'

'Of course I am. Who wouldn't be enticed by such a beautiful woman?'

I felt my cheeks warming, flushing down my neck. I took a drink of my champagne, enjoyed the strength it gave me. *I want you to kiss me again, Jonny. Kiss me and hold me.* 'What would you like to happen?'

He put down his fork and for a moment I thought he was going to take my hand but he picked up his champagne. 'I'd like to ravish you.'

'That makes two of us.'

'You've really turned me on, Emma.'

'That makes two of us,' I repeated.

He laughed, finished his champagne.

'I have a treat for you, Jonny,' I said.

'You do?'

'Maria will return shortly, to confirm that our room is ready.'

His eyes lit up. 'A room?'

I passed him the keys to Suki's jeep. 'Fetch the suitcase from the back, would you?'

Six

Jonathon

Our room wasn't any old room but one of nine themed cabins in the wooded area behind the beer garden. I'm not sure what the theme of cabin 7 was meant to be. The main feature seemed to be the life-size silverback gorilla, as tall as Emma, made of plastic but very lifelike. It wore a grass skirt, and a bright pink Hawaiian leis hung around its neck. And every shelf, cabinet, windowsill held all manner of model seagulls, ships anchors, shells, and a naval depiction of the three wise monkeys.

The bed was inviting. Big, robust, with a perfect mattress and plump pillows. The headboard was an amazing work of art, swirling metal in the shapes of vines and ivy reached upwards, almost to the ceiling, ending in the shapes of peacock feathers.

Waiting next to the bed was a side table set with more champagne. Two bottles. And a bowl of strawberries.

Emma locked the front door. She took off the wig and glasses. 'Nice place. What do you think?'

'I think, how the hell did you manage to snag such a room in the height of summer? These places are always booked out well in advance. You must be giving Maria a handsome tip.'

'Not Maria. My aunt. She booked it for me. Somewhere I could run to . . . if I didn't like you.'

'Your aunt thinks of everything.'

'She's always looked after me. Better than my own mother ever did.'

I noticed the change in her face then, a flash of something. Sadness? Insecurity? Our eyes locked. 'Champagne,' she said, 'would you do the honours?'

I went to the side table, opened one of the chilled bottles and filled two flutes. She arrived at my side and took a glass from me. 'To us,' she said, clinked my glass and downed the contents of hers in one.

'To us!' I raised my glass to her then swallowed it down. We both put our glasses on the side table at the same time. I went to refill them but her hand on my arm stopped me.

Emma

Kiss me, I thought, and he did, softly at first, his full lips on mine. And as we kissed I opened his shirt and my fingers travelled his toned chest, his nipples stiffening under my caress. And as we kissed my dress came off over my head and landed on the gorilla's arm. I popped his jeans and tugged down the zipper and they fell away and he pulled me to him, warm skin to warm skin, his growing hardness pressing into my tummy.

'Fuck me,' I said and he lifted me into his arms and his cock slid easily into me. Legs tight around his back. Arms wrapped around his shoulders. The kiss went on, slowly, gently, and with his hands gripping my ass he fucked me to shuddering oblivion and it was incredible.

I was still groaning and moaning on a post-orgasmic high as he laid me on the bed. His cold mouth touched to my pussy and the fizz of champagne flushed over me and I bucked into him, snatched the bedcover in my hands as he licked and sucked and slid a finger up my ass as I came. And it was incredible.

We showered and he washed me and I knew without any doubt that he'd done this for Heather and I loved him for it as he washed between my legs. I washed him back and brought him back to hardness and he turned me to the wall and fucked me from behind under the steaming jets of water. And it was incredible.

We drank more champagne and he nibbled strawberries from my pussy as I sucked on his cock and it was incredible.

We kissed and fucked into the afternoon. And we kissed and fucked into the evening. And it was incredible. Two souls. Two bodies so perfectly matched. Skin against skin. His taste was in my mouth. We were one, and it was incredible. It was all incredible . . . and we'd lain in a daze forever. Entwined. Holding. And it was bliss. Bliss until the haze started to clear and the undeniable niggle was back. *Mother.*

The thought of him fucking her made me feel sick. The fact that he chose not to tell me made me feel even sicker. 'What's she called?' I heard myself say and my stomach churned.

'Hmm? Who?' He stroked my hair and I almost flinched.

My heart was thudding now. '. . . Client number two.'

His grip relaxed, just a little, then he hugged me again and kissed my hair without replying.

'I mean,' I went on, 'saying *client number two* all the time is a bit of a mouthful. Simpler just to say her name, right?'

He pulled back from me, raised himself up on an elbow. 'What's brought this on?'

'Brought what on?'

'We've had a great day; we don't need to talk about work. Besides, client confidentiality, Emma. I can't disclose names. You know that.'

'You told me Barry's name.'

'I told you it wasn't his real name. Anyway, you aren't in competition with anyone. There's no need to continue bringing up client number two.'

'You started it. You're the one that kept bringing her up.'

'Not today I haven't.'

That was true, but she was there, in my mind, and he was there, fucking her, making her scream, making her happy. 'Still,' I said, 'seems to me that you must really like her.'

'Like her? She's a client. Nothing more than that. I'm sorry if I went on about her. Listen, Emma, you are far better than client number two, or any other client come to that.'

'Better?'

'Yes.'

'In what way?' Now I was sounding needy. I needed to shut the fuck up.

His reply came without hesitation. 'You turn me on.'

'And the others don't?'

'Exactly that.'

He stared at me, a stern look. I was spoiling the mood. Spoiling the day. But I wanted honesty. Maybe I should just ask him outright, call him out on it. Or maybe I should shut my needy mouth and sleep on it. I sighed and rested my head on his chest.

Jonathon

It had been one hell of a day. We'd kissed until our lips were sore and Emma's lovely mouth was stubble-rashed, and then we'd kissed some more. We'd fucked every which way until we were spent and the day had felt like a dream until she mentioned client number two.

In the darkness of the room, she was curled in to me, head on my chest, arm draped over me, her breasts pressed against my side, one leg hitched up over mine. The room smelled of her, and of champagne and strawberries and sex. I stroked her hair. She was beautiful. And she was snoring. And I felt awful about her mother. I almost wanted to wake her up and confess all, until my phone pinged on the side table. Careful not to wake Emma, I reached for my phone. And when I saw the email from Andy Morgan I could barely believe it . . .

Email from: A. Morgan@ClubExplicit

Subject: Re: Info.

Hey Jonathon,

Arnold Winters is a blacklisted piece of shit. His first warning was for accosting one of our bar staff. His second warning was for trying to join a scene on stage. He actually assaulted one of the girls. I finally cancelled his membership when he was found importuning in the men's toilets. Offering cash for favours. He's nothing but trouble. Don't go anywhere near.

Hope you're well. Faye says hi and to drop in sometime!

Andy.

. . . and the ugly secret that was Emma's mother had suddenly doubled in size. I lay awake for a good while, weighing up my options as Emma snored on. *I'm sorry to tell you, Emma, but it appears your dirty old man can't keep his hands to himself. And he likes men. He likes them so much he doesn't mind paying for them. Oh, and by the way, client number two, let's call her Mom.*

What would she do? Would she go ballistic, at them, for being filthy hypocritical bastards and tell them to stick the wedding? Or ballistic at me for interfering and embarrassing her? I didn't like the idea of letting her down and upsetting her, or of facing her wrath.

But there was also her betrothed. William Ripley. Jessica Jones hadn't got back to me yet. I wrote Jessica a polite reminder, told her it was urgent... *a matter of life and death* I added, thinking that perhaps it really was. If Jessica came back with something, I'd add it to the murky pot and see how things stood then. Feeling slightly relieved that I didn't yet have to reveal anything to Emma Jane, I kissed her head, pulled the covers over us, and held her.

Chapter Thirteen

The Cabin

DAY FIVE

Emma

With a thumping head, I opened my eyes to sunlight streaming through the blinds and the first thing I saw was his cock standing proud, the covers draped around it. The next thing I saw was my mother sitting on it. I closed my eyes against the bright sunlight. But with my eyes closed the image of my mother cackling while she fucked him remained stronger than ever.

My head was on his chest, my legs touching his legs, warm beneath the covers. I could wake up like this every day, and I'd see to his morning glory whichever way he fancied. I could do that with him. But I knew that was never going to happen. I knew that only too well in the cold light of day. Jonathon Gold wasn't exactly swooning over me. Wasn't exactly being honest with me. But why should he be? He was getting paid for fucking me. It was his *work* and I was his customer. That's all. I glanced up at his sleeping face. Head to one side, hair a mess, mouth open. I wondered if he was dreaming, and if in future he might dream about me and the things we'd done together.

Snippets of a dark dream started coming back to me. The church dream again – *We are gathered here today* – barred windows, no escape, bells ringing, and the flash of cameras capturing the happy couple. I shivered. I needed the loo. I slipped quietly from the bed and tilted the blinds on the way to the bathroom.

I drew a glass of water and poured it in one end as I sat and pissed out the other. Now I felt miserable. Life can be so cruel sometimes, and people, they can be cruel. Selfish. *Dishonest.*

But then I thought of Aunt Fee. She'd had some tough times. Look at her now, enjoying life to the max. I imagined her standing before me in her hippie dress, bangles rattling as she wagged a finger. *Get up off of your lazy arse and do something about it, lady. Life's too short and all that. Tell the man that you love him! Tell him!* Did I love him? What was love, anyway? A fancy? A passing attraction? Infatuation? Who wouldn't be infatuated with Jonathon Gold? I remembered the spark in Maria's eye. One click of his fingers and she would have fucked him.

I thought about William. I would marry him and fuck him on a Friday and everyone would be happy, and I'd make the best of it stuck in an old vicarage with my horses miles away at my dirty mother's house. In my mind I stood William Ripley next to Jonathon Gold. Chalk and cheese didn't even come close.

I imagined myself next to Jonathon. We looked pretty good as a couple, even though I said so myself. Part of me wanted to forget what lay ahead, forget that I was getting married to a prick and instead go out there and fuck Jonny Gold awake. But I couldn't, my mother was brooding in mind like an old crow.

Without flushing, I tiptoed to the bathroom door. He was still in the same position, asleep and with his morning glory standing proud. I wrapped a bathrobe around me and went soundlessly to the bed, allowed my eyes to take him in, his toned chest, the V of his tattooed hips, and of course his beautiful cock. He gave a sniff, and his hand travelled down his stomach, fingers scratching here and there, a grunt then he stilled, mouth open, breathing softly.

I sat gently on the bed and stared at him.

Jonathon

I felt her moving. Felt the cool draught down my side as she left the bed. I'd been dreaming. Of Heather. Blonde hair so bright. Dressed in black. I kept my eyes closed, willed sleep to return. And the dream continued for a few more frames, where I felt that I could control it, make it any dream I wanted. Emma flickered. In blue. She thrashed my stomach with a crop, then so did Heather. Thrash, thrash. Then it was gone. The sound of Emma peeing in the bathroom.

I realised I had a hard on. Nothing unusual there, though. I also realised that I stunk. Of old sex. Of Emma. And my head was a bit thick from the champagne; my mouth dryer than a nun's cunt. I wondered if there would be an email waiting from Jessica Jones. Then I sensed Emma. She was watching me. I gave a sniff, ran my hand down my stomach and gave it a scratch, then I went still. I felt the mattress dip, a careful and slow dip. I felt her warmth near my leg and waited for her touch. Waited for her fingers to wrap around my cock, for her lips to suck me in, for her to climb on top and fuck me. But she didn't touch me at all. Only silence and stillness and the warmth of her next to my leg.

I opened my eyes to see her sitting there wrapped in a bathrobe. She looked like shit, almost sickly. I sensed that all was not well in Emma Jane's world. 'Good morning,' I said, 'how are you this morning?'

'A thick head,' she said and rubbed her temples.

'Mine too. But we had a good time.'

Silence. Her eyes downcast.

'Are you all right?' I asked and pulled the covers over my waning hard on.

She let out a sigh. 'Yeah. Just been thinking . . . about things.'

'Things?'

Another hesitation. 'Oh, you know, my time with you is almost up, then . . .'

'Ah. The wedding?'

'Yeah. The wedding.'

'Don't do it,' I said, sitting up and placing a hand on her shoulder. 'You deserve better, Emma.' She looked as though she wanted to say something but couldn't.

She made us coffee and we sat on the bed to drink it. 'What would you like to do today?' she asked.

I had the strangest feeling that I was about to get the brush off. I don't know why or how exactly but I know that the vibe of connection I'd felt yesterday wasn't quite there. I lifted her chin with my fingers and kissed her soft lips. She kissed me back, but pulled away before the kiss could develop any further.

'Well?' she said. 'If the choice was yours, what would you do today?'

It felt like the six-million-dollar question. So I told her what I truly felt, 'I would happily revisit the sheep pen, and sit on the wall with you and stare at the fields, and play footsie over lunch, that was so much fun. And fuck you in my arms. It was a great day, but really, Emma, the choice is yours.'

'It was a great day,' she said, as if reminiscing about something she could never have again. 'And I loved sleeping with you . . . proper sleeping, I mean. That was nice.'

'I loved it too. All of it. And I can't wait for today. We can do anything you want, Emma.'

'Okay,' she said, taking our coffee cups to the side table. 'There is something.'

Emma

A part of me didn't want to do this. Maybe I was happy with the memories I already had. Or maybe I was scared of failing. Scared of not being up to my mother's dirty standards. But I was going to try. A final empowered fling. He almost looked terrified when I pulled two pairs of shackles from the suitcase. 'It's all right, Jonny,' I said, a forcefulness in my tone that wasn't intentional. 'Get on the bed.'

I puffed pillows around his back and had him lying against the headboard, arms raised, shackled at the wrists and the shackles attached to the swirling metal. I raised his knees and opened his legs and sat on the bed in front of him, my legs locked underneath his. 'You're fucking gorgeous, you know that?' I said.

'Say that to the mirror,' he said, looking slightly worried.

His cock was almost flaccid now, hanging over his balls. 'Make it hard for me,' I said. He looked at me, smiled an unsure smile. 'Can you do that? Without me touching it?' I opened my robe and cupped my breasts, squeezed them, coaxed my nipples into hardness. His cock gave a little twitch.

I leaned back on one elbow, opened my robe and slipped a hand between my legs, pushed through my damp folds and rubbed myself to slickness. I drew my wet fingers into my mouth and sucked them clean.

His cock was starting to rise before my eyes. I rolled from the bed, leant over him and took his cock in my mouth and sucked him to hardness before stepping back.

'Where are you going?' he said as I picked up the suitcase.

There was a heartbeat – just a heartbeat – where I nearly walked. There and then. I saw myself getting dressed, ignoring his pleas. Saw myself striding back to Suki's jeep and getting the hell out. But I didn't. I didn't say a word as I carried the suitcase into the en suite.

Jonathon

I felt the rush of blood when I saw her, when she stepped from the bathroom. I recognised the playsuit. The finest Italian leather, all straps and chains and O-rings, cut away at the sides up past the hip and a low-hanging tunic-style front only just hid her pussy. She'd slicked her hair back and applied makeup; deep red lips and sultry eyes. In one hand – a flogger. I couldn't take my eyes off her.

She cocked her head. 'Speechless?'

'Hot stuff,' I said, 'you look stunning, Emma. Really stunning.' I tugged at my shackles. 'Let me free.'

She stepped up to the bed and dangled the flogger's leather tresses over my cock before giving it a nudge with the handle. 'Ever had your dick whipped, Jonny? Stupid question. Course you have.'

I gritted my teeth as she pulled back and swung the flogger and I grunted as the tresses connected across my thigh, some catching around the base of my cock. She tugged it away and struck again. My other thigh this time and I yelped as my balls were hit. 'Fuck!'

'Quiet,' she said, reached under me and gripped my balls. She brought her lips to mine and kissed me, softly. I could taste the lipstick.

And I could smell her perfume; the lightest touch of something exotic. Our tongues met and I sank into the kiss, my cock stiffening as she gently squeezed my balls. Then she let go, stroked her fingers up my stomach, and as she pulled her lips from mine she slipped two fingers into my mouth. I sucked them in, scraped them with my teeth and managed not to gag as she pushed them to the back of my throat.

'You're good,' she said, pulling her fingers away and sucking them clean. She placed the flogger on the bed, held on to my shoulders and climbed onto the bed, forcing my head against the metal rails as she leant into me. She lifted the front of the leather tunic and pushed her pussy into my face.

Emma

I didn't think he could breathe but I didn't care. To have him shackled and at my whim, to have his mouth pressed into me, sucking, tonguing; the control felt so liberating. I ground into him, his nose catching my clit over and over, his tongue probing, his teeth pulling at my lips, and I rode it out, grunting and thrusting until I came, pushing onto him until the shuddering stopped.

When I pulled away he was gasping for breath. I decided that the time it took me to turn around and present him with my ass would be enough for him to get his breath. I turned, one foot either side of his legs and planted my hands on his knees before slowly reversing onto his face.

His tongue found my asshole straight away and the sensation sent tickling pulses of pleasure right through me. I rubbed myself up and down on him, my asshole catching his nose and it felt good. No, better than good. It felt dirty – filthy dirty and empowered and fucking magnificent.

I pulled away and fell to the bed between his legs, giggling. Again he was catching his breath, his face glistening with my juices. He grinned at me and I grinned back.

'Let me free.' He rattled his shackles.

'No.' I got onto my knees between his legs and took his cock into my mouth and sucked it back to hardness before sitting cross-legged and hitching up his knees.

I showed him three fingers before sliding them into my soaking wet pussy. He watched open-mouthed as I fucked myself. And I almost didn't want to stop, it felt so fucking liberating.

'You really turn me on,' he said.

'So you keep saying.'

'I mean it, Emma. Take the shackles off. You won't regret it.'

I pulled my fingers away from myself and they were thick and sticky with my juices. He opened his mouth and I pushed them inside, right inside, until his tongue had them clean.

'Please.' He rattled his shackles again, his breaths heavy. 'Look at my cock, *Mistress Six*. It's begging for you.'

'Mistress Six? I like that.' *I did like that.*

'It suits you. You look amazing. You *are* amazing. Let me go!'

'No!' I returned my fingers to my pussy, slicked them up, and took great delight in watching his gaze as I settled into position, hunched up close to his cock. One finger first, stroking the tight entrance to his ass. His cock twitched and he exhaled. When I slid my finger inside his tight little hole his head went back and he gasped. I worked it in, twisting and turning and he went with it easily, eyes closed to it, mouth hanging.

'Is that good, Jonny?'

'Fuck yes,' he said, 'but you can't do that for long.'

'I'll do it as long as I like.' I slipped a second finger in and twisted them at the same time and he jerked.

'Oh God,' he said. 'I'll come soon, if you keep doing that.'

'Good,' I said and forced a third finger into him. I pushed them in with a twist and twisted them back out. Then in again, feeling around inside and when he groaned I gave his cock a little tug.

'Do it,' he said.

'Do what?'

'Finish it. Quickly. It fucking hurts. I need to come. I'm going to come!'

I turned my three fingers into him once more and realised then how slack he was, how easily he opened up for me. Of course he could take my fingers down his throat without gagging. Of course his ass was receptive. He was experienced. God knew how many women had done this to him. I felt my lip twitch as I thought of my mother, sitting here, just like this, all dressed up and sultry and dirty as she rammed her fingers home.

'Please, Emma.'

I gave him a questioning look.

'Please, Mistress Six. Finish it.'

I showed him four fingers and didn't give him time to think as I pushed them deep inside his hot ass. Then I fucked him. Hard. And he tensed up and cried out as my hand pumped his asshole to orgasm, his cock jerking with each spasm, and each spasm brought cum spurting up his stomach and chest. I pulled my fingers away from him, grabbed his cock and squeezed the last from him.

'You were right,' I said. 'You came really quickly.'

Jonathon.

I tugged at my shackles with force. 'Will you let me go now? I so much want to fuck you.'

'So soon?'

'Give me five minutes and I'll be ready to go.'

She smiled at that, licked her dark red lips. 'And how would Jonny like to fuck?'

'Your call,' I said. 'As long as it's hard and fast, I don't fucking care.'

'Wrong answer,' she said.

I had to think about that but soon remembered. 'Emma Jane, I want to kiss your beautiful lips and pick you up and slide you onto my cock. I want to hold you in my arms and fuck you with your legs wrapped around me and your arms hanging free. I'll fuck you so hard you'll want to cry out for me to stop, but you won't. You'll ride it out and scream for me. Now, let me free.'

She was grinning. She licked her lips, made to get up on her knees. But my phone ringing on the side table stopped her in her tracks and my heart leapt.

'Ignore it,' I said. 'It'll just be work.'

'Work?'

I got the feeling I'd said the wrong thing.

'Just press the cancel button,' I said. 'They can leave a message.'

But now she was up on all fours, moving closer to the phone, staring at the caller I.D. 'I recognise that number. That's Aunt Fee's number.'

My heart almost stopped. 'She'll be checking up, that's all. Making sure you're all right.'

She looked at me, looked back at the ringing phone and picked it up.

Shit.

Emma

I pressed Accept and put the phone to my ear. 'Hello?' *Silence.* 'Aunt Fee?' The line went dead. 'She hung up.'

'Probably lost connection,' he said.

'Then she'll call back.'

'Turn it off,' he said, and rattled the shackles. 'Please, let me go and let's get back to fucking.'

Aunt Fee had maybe made a timely interruption. 'Back to fucking? Or back to work?' His eyes flashed then. He looked almost dejected. 'That's the honest truth of it, isn't it? I'm just your *work*.'

'No, Emma,' he began but I cut him off.

'It's true, Mr Gold. You've been paid to fuck me.'

He sighed. 'Technically, yes, but it didn't even cross my mind, Emma. The money, I mean. I'll give it back.'

'And why would you do that?'

'Please let me go.'

'Tell me. Why would you give up your whoring spoils?'

'That's not nice.'

'It's the truth, though. You can't deny that. And you know what, I might be a dirty slut but at least I have values.'

'Of course you have values. And you're not a slut. Let's stop this and get back to where we were. Let me go. Please, Emma.'

Now was the time. I'd had enough. 'I'm going to let you go,' I said and he looked at me with uncertainty. 'Back to your den of sex.'

'What?'

'You heard me. I'm calling you a taxi.'

'But why?'

'You can't even guess?' His eyes darted away then. He knew all right.

I laughed. At myself more than anything. 'Do you know, over the past day or two, I'd convinced myself I was actually in love with you.'

He looked at me with sad eyes, the colour draining from him.

'And I've being trying to please you, to show you how good I can be, how good *we* can be together.'

'You *were* good,' he said, 'better than good.'

'But it wasn't love at all. Because love can't become love until it's shared, until it's reciprocated. Just like a horse's love, remember? And it never was. I was just client number six. Your *work*.'

'That's not true,' he said. 'I really like you, Emma, and . . .'

'Like me?'

'Please don't call for a taxi. I don't want it to end like this.'

'How do you want it to end?'

He huffed, rattled his shackles. 'Happy,' he said, 'not with you marrying someone you don't love.'

'You have no right to preach to me about what I should and shouldn't fucking do, Jonathon. No right at all. If I'd meant anything to you, you would have told me that client number two was my own fucking mother, and that you'd fucked her.'

There was an awful silence as my words sank in. He looked gutted. 'I wanted to tell you, Emma. I really did, but . . .'

'But fucking nothing. You didn't tell me. You just kept on pointing out my filthy mother's favourite tricks. Make you feel good, did it? Fucking both mother and daughter – not to mention my fucking aunt.'

'I didn't want to hurt you.'

'Bull fucking shit, Jonathon. And don't go blaming Suki for telling me, either. She did what *you* should have done.'

'Emma, please, you're being unreasonable. Let me go and we can talk.'

'Oh? We can talk? What would you like to talk about, Mr Gold?'

'The most important thing of all,' he said. 'The wedding. Don't go through with it, Emma. You deserve better.'

'You just don't get it, do you? I can't just say *No* and walk away. You don't know my father. There'd be nowhere to hide. He'd hunt me down and hold a shotgun to my head until I said *I do*.'

'Stay with me, Emma, at my place. He won't ever get to you there.'

'Stay with you? Ah, yes, I'd make a good fucking angel, wouldn't I?'

He sighed again, rattled his shackles. 'Emma, this isn't how it's meant to be.'

'If you'd been fucking truthful with me in the first place, maybe it would be different. But you weren't.'

'I'm sorry for that.'

'My own fucking mother,' I said and was almost sick at the thought him making her come. 'Jesus!' I picked up the flogger and hurled it across the room. It thumped into a wooden seagull, knocked it flying along with a whole heap of shells that clattered to the floor.

'Emma! Look at me.'

I glared at him, heart thudding.

'Please calm down. We can talk through this.'

'Then talk,' I said, 'and start by telling me what else you're hiding.'

'What do you mean?'

'Be careful, Jonny. You had one big fucking secret, odds are you've got more. I'm not totally fucking stupid. I want the truth.'

He relaxed, arms limp in the shackles, chin on his chest, and he took a breath. He actually looked quite pathetic with his own cum drying on his chest. 'All right,' he said and looked me in the eye. 'There is something else. Undo the shackles and I'll show you.'

'Show me? Just tell me.'

'It's on my phone, Emma. It'll be easier to show you.'

Jonathon

She undid the shackles and stepped back quickly. I made a move towards her but she stepped back again.

'Don't,' she said, 'just show me what you've got to show me.'

'Please be warned,' I said, 'what you're about to see is not very nice. You might want to sit down.'

She held out a hand. 'I'm a big girl. Show me.'

I picked up my phone and quickly checked new emails but there was still no reply from Jessica Jones. I found Andy Morgan's email and handed the phone to Emma.

She read the email, looked up at me, then back to the email and read it again. When she looked up again she'd gone white as snow. She threw the phone at me and ran to the bathroom, slamming the door behind her.

Great heaving sobs were followed by great heaving retches echoing around the en suite as the poor girl puked her guts up. I felt helpless. And a bastard. She was right, I should have been truthful from the start. I found some wipes, cleaned myself, pulled on my jeans and shirt.

I made us some coffee and sat on the bed and waited and felt like the stupidest man on the planet.

When she finally unlocked the door and stepped back into the room she was in her bathrobe, makeup removed, hair ruffled. She had her phone in her hand. 'Your taxi will be at reception in ten minutes,' she said.

'I don't want to go back, Emma. Not without you. We can sort this out.'

The look she gave me wasn't the one of acceptance I'd hoped for. Her eyes were dark, bloodshot. 'Just what the fuck was that email all about?'

'I'm sorry,' I said, 'I was doing some digging, thought if I could find something on your father . . .'

'That that would be enough for me to tell him to shove the wedding up his arse?'

'Yes. If you like.'

'You have no idea. No idea, Jonathon. He'd hound you, report you, reveal you, and before you could blink he'd close you down.'

'You're right. I'm sorry. Perhaps I should have talked with you first.'

'Too late for that, though, isn't it? While I've been fawning at your feet and giving you my heart you've been dancing in the dark behind my back like a private fucking detective. Who else have you been digging the dirt on? Me? You been searching for my skeletons? Because I've got fucking plenty, only you already fucking know about them because I was always honest with you.'

'No, Emma. I did no digging where you were concerned.'

'William then. You must have went sniffing down that sorry path.'

I nodded. 'I asked questions, yes, but I heard nothing back. Please, Emma, let's rewind, start this again, we can sort things out.'

'It's already sorted. Your taxi will be here any minute.'

'Please, come back with me.'

'I've had enough, Jonathon. I've decided to accept my fate and I suggest you accept yours.'

'And what is my fate exactly? I want you, Emma.'

She shook her head. 'I'll call you, after the wedding, once the dust settles.'

'After the wedding?'

'Hell yes. If I'm going to live a life of purgatory in a stuffy old vicarage, I'm going to need an outlet and you still owe *this* client a whole day.'

I should have been able to smile at that but I couldn't. 'This is all wrong, Emma.'

Her phone rang. She answered it, said thanks, hung up. 'Your taxi. I'll see you.' She went to the door and swung it wide. I wanted to hug her but there was no denying the way she held the door like a shield.

'Emma, please don't do this.'

'It's done.'

Chapter Fourteen

Jessica's Email

Jonathon

I was almost sick in the taxi on the ride home; the sounds of Emma retching in the en suite still fresh in my mind didn't help. I'd let her down; let myself down. I felt like the world's biggest loser.

In fact, I felt worse than that. I felt saddened by the loss of her. She'd gone from me, just like that. Her tear-filled eyes the last thing I saw as the door closed on me. And I'd walked away on hazy autopilot, all the way through reception and into the waiting taxi, knowing that she was crying.

I had the taxi driver drop me at the gates. I didn't glance to the gatehouse to see who was on security, I just waved a hand and walked on past as the gates slid open. I stepped through onto the gravel drive and the gates closed behind me with a definitive thud. And as I stood there under the baking sun, the driveway weaving through the lawns into the distance, there were no birds singing, no insects buzzing. The place felt dead. Felt like work . . . not home.

I took out my phone, hoping for a text or a call from Emma, but of course she didn't have my number. I had hers on file, though. I walked up the long drive, cursing myself for not letting the taxi take me to the house, cursing the sun for being too hot, and cursing the fact that a girl in a white skirt and polo shirt was running to meet me. Suki was the last person I wanted to see right now. She'd obviously spotted me on the CCTV. By the time we met, the sweat was running down my face.

'Where's Miss Emma? Has something happened?'

I had the urge to strangle her, the rise of temper, blood boiling. 'Leave it,' I said, and walked on by.

I hadn't quite reached the steps when she was tugging at my arm. I shrugged her off. She looked up at me like a frightened child.

'Please, Mr Gold. Is Miss Emma okay?'

I felt my nostrils flaring, felt something that was too close to hate to be anywhere near being a good thing but I couldn't stop myself. 'Miss Emma is *mightily* pissed off with me,' I said. 'Miss Emma didn't take kindly to the fact that client number two is her own fucking mother.'

'Oh.' Suki visibly swallowed. 'Is she coming back?'

'If you hadn't opened your big mouth and spilled secrets you weren't at liberty to spill, then maybe she'd still be here. You had no right, Suki. No right at all.'

A tear ran down her cheek. 'I'm sorry, so sorry,' she whimpered, and clasped her hands to her face.

'Get out of my sight,' I said, and walked away.

I heard her apologising again but didn't look back.

I heard her sobbing but didn't look back.

I heard her running off but didn't look back.

Once in my office I took off my shirt, wiped my face and chest with it and threw it to one side. I fired up the PC, poured myself a full tumbler of whisky, took a generous drink, and located Emma's number. I entered it into my phone.

Should I ring her and apologise?

Or send a text?

I'm sorry I fucked your mother. I'm sorry I didn't tell you. Can we forget all this and start again?

But I knew that not any of that would cut it with Emma. Shit. I'd truly fucked up.

I slugged back the whisky, poured another, slugged that back too, and slammed the glass down so hard I was surprised it didn't smash.

I needed the gym. I left my office and headed through to the back of the house and down the stairs, not meeting a single angel on the way. I thought maybe Suki had warned them off.

No wraps. No gloves. I laced into the punch bag like there was no fucking tomorrow.

Emma

I'd cried for an hour, curled up on the bed and wrapped in the covers heavy with his smell. The whole place smelled of him and so did I. So I'd showered, hands on the wall and head under the steaming jets, only this time he wasn't behind me fucking me or washing me, and I cried some more; cried until I was retching; cried until I had to force the tears to stop. Fucking hell.

What a fool I'd been. Jonathon Gold was nothing but a fantasy. And I probably wasn't the first client to fall in love with him. Who could resist his charm, his looks, his prowess, his kind heart? If only *honesty* was on his list of attributes.

I sat on my bed with a coffee in one hand and my phone in the other, and I even managed a smile at his picture, those twinkling eyes, those dimples when he grinned. The memory of where his toes were at the time brought involuntary sparks down below. Should I call him? Say sorry? *Sorry for being such a needy wuss, Jonny, but love kinda does that to a girl . . . I'm sorry for my slut mother, too. If you'd like to deliver her head to me on a platter, I might just fucking forgive you.*

No, of course I couldn't ring him. He didn't *love* me. I'd made myself look stupid. Needy and stupid. I couldn't ring Aunt Fee, either. If I did she'd jump on the next plane home and stick her nose in where it wasn't wanted. I'd wait here until tomorrow, until she arrived to collect me and show off my wedding dress. The very thought made my stomach turn.

There *was* someone I needed to ring, though.

I held his business card in trembling fingers as I typed his number into my phone, hoping to God that he wouldn't answer it. Where would he be right now? Probably brooding, drinking, blaming everyone but himself. I rang the number and pressed my phone to my ear to stop my hand from shaking.

The call was picked up on the third ring and I held my breath, ready to disconnect if it was him.

'Gold Escort Services, Annabelle speaking. How may I help you?'

I breathed out the relief on hearing Annabelle's voice. 'May I speak with Suki please?'

Jonathon

I blamed the whisky, of course. Punching a bag with bare fists doesn't take long to bloody your knuckles. Doesn't take long until you're hugging the bag and sobbing like a baby. I'd locked myself away in one of the wet rooms and paced under the shower jets until all the blood and sweat and tears had gone.

Now I was back at my desk, another whisky poured, staring at Emma's image on my phone. I sent the image to my PC and she smiled back at me as large as life. I touched my fingers to her lips and felt the need to kiss them again. Part of me wanted to jump in the car, knock on her cabin door with a huge bouquet of flowers, beg her forgiveness. But I knew it was too soon, that Emma would need space. More than anything I hoped she might come around to seeing things from my perspective and realise I was in a truly awkward position regarding her mother. That we could forget what happened and tomorrow she would turn up for her final day of fun and I'd get to hold her and kiss her again.

One can hope, right? I decided the best thing to do today was to send her a text message.

I picked up my phone. Fumbled with the keys. Unsure of what to say. Said too much. Delete, delete, delete. Tried again. And again. And eventually settled on just three words.

I made a wish to the Good Fairy – just like Heather used to do – and pressed Send.

Emma

I left the cabin door wide open so that I wouldn't have to answer it, and I sat on the bed cross-legged with my phone in one hand and Suki's sunglasses and the keys to her jeep in the other. I'd placed the borrowed costume in a refuse sack, along with the blonde wig, and left it by the door.

I heard the roll of suitcase wheels on the pathway, saw her shadow approaching. Her shadow paused and my heart was already too loud.

'Come in,' I said and the shadow was replaced by Suki herself, pulling my suitcase behind her. She'd been crying; eyes red and puffy.

She took a step forward but when I held up a hand to stop her she ignored it and joined me on the bed. She hugged me and sobbed into my shoulder and that was all it took. I hugged her back and we sobbed together until eventually she pulled away and wiped damp hair from my face.

'Miss Emma,' she said, her bottom lip trembling, 'please come back with me.'

I shook my head *No*, and wiped my tears away. 'I can't.'

'Can't or won't?' she sniffed, 'Miss Emma, this is too important to let go.'

'This? What exactly is *this*, Suki?'

She looked at me with such sad eyes.

I drew a breath, filled myself with bravado. 'I fucked Mr Gold. For money. And now I'm done. End of. That's what *this* is.'

'You still have one more day. Please come for last day.'

Despite the small laugh that left my lips, the idea wasn't instantly dismissed. I saw myself turning up in the morning, and had the feeling *he'd* do whatever I dammed well wanted to do. I pictured Suki's Starfish toy strapped around my hips, and me taking up position behind Jonathon Gold's shackled ass. And I'd let him have it, fuck him hard as he screamed for me to stop. But I wouldn't stop. I'd fuck him raw until he screamed out loud that he *loved* me. That he really *wanted* me. That he . . .

'Miss Emma?'

I realised that my breaths were heavy. I was almost panting.

My phone beeped and my heart froze. I even heard Suki gasp. We both knew who it would be.

I picked up my phone with a trembling hand.

Text message. Number unknown.

My thumb hovered over the button to open the message and then I pressed it. But the three little words I saw were not the three little words I'd hoped for.

`I'm Sorry. Jon. xx`

I stared at the words. Meaningless words. The man had no emotion. The man had no idea.

I deleted the message.

'Miss Emma?'

I looked into her hopeful eyes.

'Was that Mr Gold?'

'Spam,' I lied, and threw the phone on the bed.

'Please come tomorrow,' she persisted, 'please talk with Mr Gold. I know you can work it out.'

I shook my head again. 'There's nothing to work out. I was nothing but a paying client. Just like my whoring mother . . . I'm no better.'

'That's not true.'

'It's very much the truth, Suki.'

'But you have one more day, Miss Emma. Please come.'

'You can tell Mr Gold to stick it up his arse and swivel.'

Her lip started quivering again. I sighed and took her hands. 'Suki I'm sorry. But I can't. I just can't.'

'I'm already missing you so bad,' she said and burst into tears.

I hugged her to me and stroked her hair. I was already missing her, too. God this was so fucking hard. 'Look at me,' I said and tilted her face to mine. 'I know that you would love nothing more than for me and Jonathon to hit it off –'

'But you did hit it off, Miss Emma. You–'

I placed a finger to her lips. 'Please, Suki. Please understand that there's something I must do. Something I don't want to do but can't avoid.'

'Getting married?'

'Yes.'

'How can I understand that. You said you don't love fiancé. That makes no sense.'

'Sometimes, Suki, it's not about love . . . or at least true *love*-love. Sometimes it's about family, and doing what's best for them–'

'I don't believe that, Miss Emma. How can marrying a man you not like be best for anyone. That not right at all.'

She wasn't stupid, of course she wasn't. 'Suki, if I don't go ahead and marry William Ripley next Saturday, all hell will break loose. Daddy will lose millions and the potential for millions more. And I would be cast out and left with nothing.'

'Maybe that good idea,' she said, 'having nothing is better than being forced into something you don't want to do. Maybe . . . maybe,' she looked at me with fear in her eyes, 'maybe you just a coward.'

Ouch! I felt myself shrinking before her eyes. I bit my tongue and turned away. 'You wouldn't understand,' I said. 'Let's just leave it at that.'

'Miss Emma?'

I turned to look at her.

'I might not really understand,' she said, 'but I do understand two things.'

I think I knew what was coming.

'I understand that you love Mr Gold.'

'No, Suki. I fucked the man for fun, for money. That is all.'

'And you fell for him.'

'I . . . I like him, yes, but–'

'You love him. It's in your eyes every time you look at him, Miss Emma. You can't trick the eyes.'

'I . . . *lust*, more like . . . I–'

'And the second thing I understand is that Mr Gold loves you, too.'

The laugh that escaped me sounded fake, forced, embarrassingly so. 'Told you this, did he? Because he certainly didn't let on to me.'

'No, Miss Emma, I see his eyes, too. The way he takes you in. The way he watches out for you. The way he absorbs you and considers you. I never see Mr Gold like that since . . . since Heather died.'

Ouch again. I'd seen it in his eyes, too. Of course I had. My heart ached for him, but I couldn't go down that path. Instead I picked up Suki's sunglasses and her keys from the bed and handed them to her.

'Please forgive him,' she said, 'he didn't mean to keep client number two a secret from you. He just didn't want to hurt you.'

'If Mr Gold truly loved me then he would tell me so, and he'd sweep me off my feet. But he didn't and he hasn't and I guess he never will. Someone will come along for him, I'm sure. Someone more worthy of him than a whore like me. So please just leave it there and we'll–' She was sobbing again. 'Suki, please, you're not making this any easier.'

'I want to see you happy,' she sniffed. 'You're my friend.'

'And you're mine, Suki.' I hugged her again. 'Listen, if you really want to see me happy you must continue being a good friend and let me do what I have to do.'

'Get married to a prick?'

'Yes. Exactly that.'

She sighed, dug her hand into her pocket and pulled out my engagement ring. She appeared to think twice about giving it to me, and instead she put it on the bedside table. She placed her sunglasses over her puffy-red eyes, walked to the door and picked up the bag with the costume inside.

'Why don't you come?' I said before she walked out the door.

She stopped and looked at me.

'To the wedding. I'm serious, Suki. I could do with a real friend there. For support.'

She nodded once before walking away.

Jonathon

I was at my desk, staring at Andy Morgan's email on the monitor.

Email from: A. Morgan@ClubExplicit

Subject: Re: Info.

Hey Jonathon,

Arnold Winters is a blacklisted piece of shit. His first warning was for accosting one of our bar staff. His second warning was for trying to join a scene on stage. He actually assaulted one of the girls. I finally cancelled his membership when he was found importuning in the men's toilets. Offering cash for favours. He's nothing but trouble. Don't go anywhere near.

Hope you're well. Faye says hi and to drop in sometime!

Andy.

Bastard.

Cunt.

Slimy shitting toe-rag turd.

I wanted to ring him up, punch his haughty nose down the phone, kick him where it fucking hurts and tell him to back the fuck off. But I knew it wasn't enough. I needed something on Ripley. And Jessica Jones wasn't playing ball.

Until that is I noticed the spam folder. *36 emails.*

What an idiot!

A shiver of hope ran through me.

I clicked it open and there it was:

Email from: J.Jones@Berryhub

Subject: Re: Info.

I hovered the cursor over it, my heart pounding. Fuck. Please let the dirty bastard be guilty of something terrible. Please give me enough to destroy his sordid little world. I closed my eyes and double clicked.

Please . . . please . . . please . . .

I opened my eyes, saw the words, read them and read again.

And read them one more time.

Hi Jon,

You've no worries with Ripley. Got his kinks like anyone else, but he's clean as a whistle.

Take care, my lovely,

Jess x

And that was that. Clean as a bastard whistle.

The hope I'd felt was gone.

I put my elbows on the desk and my head in my hands, and didn't shift when the knock came at the door. 'Come!' I shouted.

It was Suki. She arrived at my desk pushing her sunglasses on top of her head to reveal eyes that had shed many tears.

'How was she?'

Suki shrugged. 'Sad. In denial. Determined.'

'Determined?'

She sighed. 'To get married.'

'She's not coming back?'

'No.'

She glared at me. If looks could kill I'd be mortally wounded. 'What?'

'You,' she said.

'Me?'

'Grow a pair, Mr Gold.'

'And do what exactly?'

'Sweep her off her feet.'

'I already tried that.'

'Maybe you not try hard enough.'

I beckoned her around the desk, brought up Andy Morgan's email.

Suki read through it. 'What's im-por-tuning?'

'Exactly what it says. Offering cash for favours in the men's toilets.'

'Favours?'

'Yeah, favours. Jack me off and I'll give you fifty. Take me in the cubicle and suck my dick and I'll give you a hundred. Those kinds of favours.'

'And that's Miss Emma's father?'

'Yes.'

'Oh my God,' she said. 'Does Miss Emma know?'

'Yes. I showed her the email.'

'And it didn't make any difference, Suki. Her father likes a bit of filthy fun, albeit with other men. It's his business, his private life, not Emma's business at all.'

'What about fiancé? Did you dig dirt on him too?'

I showed her Jessica's email. 'Nothing. Clean as a whistle.'

She touched a hand to my shoulder and sighed. 'Maybe it not dirt you should be digging for.'

'Then what?'

'Maybe you should be digging inside yourself and telling her how you truly feel. Sweep her off her feet, Mr Gold. That's what she wants. That's what she needs.'

'A knight in shining armour, galloping to her rescue on a white charger?'

'Yes.'

I laughed.

'She invited me to the wedding.'

My stomach turned at her words.

'Will you come with me?'

'I really don't think that's a good idea, Suki.'

She gave my shoulder a squeeze and left without another word.

I switched the computer to screensaver, Emma in her yellow dress, the blonde wig in her hand, her auburn hair ruffled, cheeks flushed and eyes alive with arousal as my toes had played with her beneath the table. I wanted more of that, more of her. I wanted Emma Jane Winters so much.

Chapter Fifteen

Dying Roses

DAY SIX

Jonathon

I had Annabelle cancel all appointments. Every single one. I even sent Barry home. It made a change to see him pissed-off instead of pissed-on.

I was tired of it. The sex. The kinks. The BDSM. I needed a break.

The weather had changed today, as if in tune with my mood. Grey clouds, spits of rain, and a chilly breeze that seemed determined to remove the last petals from Heather's roses. They'd bloomed well in the spring, a dazzling display of black and white along the back wall of the garden. *Like a sleeping Dalmatian*, Heather used to say. She would never deadhead them in an attempt for more attractive blooms. *Let them find their own beauty, nature's more adept than a pair of secateurs.*

Heather liked to watch them wither and die; liked to watch the petals fall. Each stage of their lives was beautiful to her. And come Autumn they'd bloom once more, and they'd be beautiful again.

I shivered as the breeze gusted and rain spots hit my face and my bare arms. I'd been here all morning, thinking of Heather and of

Emma, how similar they were, not in looks – Heather was tall and blonde, Emma short with auburn hair – but in spirit. They both had that determination in their hearts, and now Emma Jane was determined to marry someone she clearly shouldn't.

I'd hoped she'd turn up today. I'd purposely put Suki on reception. If Emma called I was to be informed immediately. I checked my phone. It was gone noon. No text message, no phone call. She wasn't coming. 'Screwed this up, didn't I?' I told the dying roses, and Heather was there by my side, her head on my shoulder, arms holding mine. And the idea was comforting, the feel of Heather's warmth, her softness.

I closed my eyes to it. That feeling of being there, of being needed, of being together, of . . . *love.*

Ring her, said the voice in my ear. And say what? And what if she totally flips at me again? I would send another text.

Emma

I'd had a fitful night's sleep, reliving Jonathon Gold in my dreams. The way he'd touched me so intimately on the couch in his office when we'd only just met. And how I'd gladly let him. The way he'd spanked me on the loveseat, thrashed me in shackles, guided me through the round room before I'd gushed for him. And how I'd gladly done all those things. But the one dream, the one that felt realest of all, was that first day, when he came to my room and held me. Fucked me in his arms and held me. I remember that time better than any other. The feel of him. His warmth. His protection. A feeling to savour; a feeling of . . . love.

He was here now, on the bed by my side, his head on my shoulder. I closed my eyes to it, savoured it. There was a man I could love forever.

I knew that. But I knew it could never be. I would marry William Ripley, make Daddy rich. *For the sake of the family,* Mother's voice in my ear. A shudder ran through me, unbidden thoughts of her riding Jonathon Gold. I cast the thoughts away. If I went down that route, I'd end up puking again.

It was time to text Aunt Fee. She'd be at the airport now.

I thought of what to say, then decided to keep it simple. I typed it out,

> Hey! No need to pick me up. Am already at the Crab & Lobster. Can't wait to see you xxx

Was that okay? I thought it was. As soon as I'd send it I'd turn my phone off. I didn't want twenty questions over the phone, it'll be bad enough when she gets here.

I read the text again, then pressed Send.

I was about to turn my phone off when it beeped.

1 New Message – number unknown.

I knew it was him. My hand started shaking. I opened up the message. Short and sweet.

Just three little words,

> I miss you xx

I turned the phone off and threw it to the bed.

Jonathon

The tears came from nowhere. Real tears. Real gut-wrenching unstoppable sobs. My legs buckled and I fell to my knees, cried into my hands. Cried until I was gasping for breath and the wind picked up and squalled the petals around me, a black and white storm of miserable beauty.

God how I wished she was here, really here, not just in spirit. I knew I would never stop feeling her. Knew I would never stop loving her. But I also knew I should move on, and that the one girl that had truly captured my heart wasn't here. I'd screwed up, with no idea of how I could put that right.

I wiped my face, got to my feet, and left the dying roses behind. The loveseat was wet with rain but I didn't care. They say reflecting on the past is good therapy. Good for being thankful for what you've got. But I was reflecting two pasts. Life with Heather – a love gone. And my short time with Emma. Love extinguished before it could even get started.

Did I love her? I loved what she did to me. I loved that I couldn't help myself when she was with me. How I'd brought her off on that couch. How I'd followed her to her room and shaved her and fucked her in my arms. She made me break my own rules. No one had done that before. No one.

My phone ringing in my shirt pocket made my leap to my feet. I yanked it out, hoping to see her name on the caller ID. But it wasn't Emma.

Fiona.

Shit.

I almost turned the phone off. But I thought better of it. I knew how strongminded she could be – just like her niece.

I pressed Accept and switched it to loudspeaker.

'Hello,' I said, staring at the phone in my hand.

'Jonathon?'

'Yes.'

'What the hell have you done?'

Now my heart was thumping.

'Jonathon? Speak to me!' Fiona's voice echoed around the garden.

'I haven't *done* anything.'

'So it would seem. My poor niece is beside herself. You've broken her heart.'

I took a breath, tried to still my heart before I broke that too.

'Jonathon!'

'There's no need to shout. I'm still here.'

An exasperated sigh. 'Jonathon, look, I know things haven't gone quite to plan, but–'

'To plan? What plan?'

Silence.

'What plan?'

Another sigh. 'I'll come straight out with it. She loves you, you know. Do you love her?'

Do I? 'We only just met.'

'Answer me this, then. How many cocks did she take?'

Straight to the point as ever. 'What do you mean?'

'Angels, how many angels fucked her?'

'None.'

'Not even in the round room?'

'No, not even there.'

'Don't you think that a little odd?'

'Odd?'

'I remember my first time in that dark corridor, Jonathon. And I remember it well. I was groped and probed and sucked, but above all I'd taken five dicks before I'd got to the end.'

She was right. 'And your point is?'

'My point is, *yours* is the only dick she's had! Is that correct?'

'And?'

Another sigh. 'It means you wanted her for yourself.'

She had a point. 'Maybe.'

'There is no maybe about it. I knew you two would hit it off and I was right.'

'Were you? You might have thought you were playing matchmaker, Fiona, but you're forgetting something.'

'Which is?'

'Emma isn't here. And I'm not with Emma. Your matchmaking was a nice idea but it didn't work. So let's just leave it at that.'

'No! Jonathon! Listen to me–'

I hung up, turned the phone off, and slumped back to the damp seat, cursing Fiona Bruce and her fickle ideas, and cursing myself for even answering her call. It was over. And I was done with it. As if to move me away from my damp seat and see some sense, and get back inside and get dry and warm, the heavens opened and the rain came down; big fat drops at first, a blink of lightning, a rumble of thunder.

I headed quickly down the gravel path, aiming for the archway in the wall when I heard footfalls, someone running. Suki came pelting through the arch. Soaked through and gasping for breath, she stopped before me.

'Mr Gold. You said tell you straight away if phone call.'

'Emma? Did she–'

'No, not Miss Emma. Miss Fiona.'

My heart sank into my sodden socks. 'I've just spoken to her.'

Suki drew a breath, wiped the rain from her face. Lightning blinked again and the thunder crack was loud and instant. I pulled her under the shelter of the archway. 'She said you hung up. But she had message.'

'Which was?'

'She wants to see us Monday morning. Nine o'clock sharp.'

'Us?'

Suki nodded. 'Me and you. She insisted. In your office, she said.'

'And you told her that would be okay?'

'I told her you were taking no appointments, but . . .'

'But?'

'She said . . . she said you must see her . . . *we* must see her . . . that it will be the most important meeting of your life.'

Chapter Sixteen

The most important meeting of your life

MONDAY MORNING

Jonathon

I changed the image on my PC, replacing Emma with an image of Heather's roses. One black, one white, and I sat back in my chair, resisting the urge to get the whisky bottle out. I'd sent Suki to reception to be there when Fiona arrived, and I admit to feeling nervous.

Would she bring Emma with her? I knew it was highly possible and that I could be in for a lecture from Fiona. She could be overpowering to get what she wanted. I knew that.

The most important meeting of my life.

I couldn't imagine what wrath was about to enter my office. Couldn't imagine any scenario at all that would make this the most important meeting of my life. I decided to play it cool, to comply. To listen to what she had to say, and hoped it wouldn't descend into a shouting match and inevitable tears.

The knock on the door made me shoot up straight and clasp my hands together on my desk. I didn't get chance to shout my usual invitation to enter when the door swung open, and in she strode, bangles, beads and swishing flowery dress, closing the distance between us quickly, with Suki hurrying along behind. I was strangely relieved not to see Emma.

I stood to greet her. 'Sit,' she said, and like an obedient puppy I sat back down.

She took hold of one of the two chairs I'd positioned in front of my desk and turned it to face the big screen on the back wall. She guided Suki to it and Suki duly sat, glanced at me with quizzical eyes and shrugged. Bemused, I almost shrugged back.

Fiona came and sat on the corner of my desk and looked at me. 'Her heart is broken,' she said. 'And it's your fault.'

I didn't respond. *Play it cool.*

'Does that bother you at all?'

Did it? 'Yes.'

'Good. Now, tell me what it is that you want, Jonathon?'

'What I want?'

'From this . . . this situation . . . Emma Jane. Do you want Emma Jane?'

I stared at her beguiling eyes.

'All I'm asking is for a truthful answer. It's not rocket science. Do you want her?'

I had to swallow the lump in my throat. Blink away the burning sensation behind my eyes. 'What do *you* want?' I said, and knew my words were pathetic.

She delivered the deserved sigh.

'Yes,' I said, 'I wish she was here. I wish you'd brought her with you.' And I realised that I meant it.

A smile, a slight nod. 'Then let me begin.' She shook her head at me. 'You're a shit detective, Jonathon.'

'Detective?'

‘I gave you the leads and you failed.’

‘Your leads came to nothing.’

‘On the contrary. You failed to do the adding up.’

I missed something? I felt my heart kick. ‘Go on.’

‘You heard back from Andy Morgan?’

‘Yes. A disturbing email regarding Emma’s father.’

‘Show me. On the big screen.’

I opened up my browser, found the email, and sent it to the screen on the wall.

Email from: A. Morgan@ClubExplicit

Subject: Re: Info.

Hey Jonathon,

Arnold Winters is a blacklisted piece of shit. His first warning was for accosting one of our bar staff. His second warning was for trying to join a scene on stage. He actually assaulted one of the girls. I finally cancelled his membership when he was found importuning in the men’s toilets. Offering cash for favours. He’s nothing but trouble. Don’t go anywhere near.

Hope you’re well. Faye says hi and to drop in sometime!

Andy.

‘Blacklisted piece of shit,’ she murmured as she read, ‘accosted staff, assault, importuning, *hmm . . .*’

‘Hmm?’ I guessed she had further revelations.

She looked at me. ‘Did you follow this up?’

'Follow it up? I thanked Andy for his time.'

'Right,' she said, 'if you'd pushed, dug a little deeper, you might have found out an interesting truth.'

'Which is?'

Fiona's mouth turned up into a devious smile. 'If you were to ask the incorrigible Mr Winters where he met his son-in-law to be, and his answer was a truthful one, where do think that might be?'

I raised an eyebrow. 'Club Explicit?'

'Yes. Or more precisely,' she said, 'in Club Explicit's toilets.'

I heard Suki gasp. I almost gasped myself. 'He . . .'

'Yes, Jonathon, and my source was witness to it. Arnold and William, locked in a stall, instant bum chums. Friends for life. *Scheming* friends for life.'

'That's sick,' I said.

'Real sick,' Suki agreed.

'Oh, but there's more,' Fiona said. 'You heard back from Jessica Jones?'

I nodded. 'Ripley's clean as a whistle, apparently.' I found Jessica's email and transferred it to the big screen.

Email from: J.Jones@Berryhub

Subject: Re: Info.

Hi Jon,

You've no worries with Ripley. Got his kinks like anyone else, but he's clean as a whistle.

Take care, my lovely,

Jess x

'Don't tell me,' I said, 'I should have dug deeper?'

'You should have done some adding up, detective.'

'Adding up?'

'When you were digging, you came across photographs of William Ripley?'

'Of course.'

'Show me. On your monitor.'

She came around my desk to stand beside me. I went to my saved images, the folder I'd named TWATS, and opened it. Six images of Ripley. Six images of Emma's mother and father.

'That one,' Fiona's finger landed on a sharp image of Ripley. He was side on, glass of wine in his hand, talking to a priest at what looked like a tea party of some sort. 'That's a good likeness. Now, send it to the big screen and watch.'

I right-clicked the image and sent it over. It took a moment or two to load in, but when it did, and Ripley was there large as life, Suki's chair scraped the floor and she stood up.

'Holy shit!' she said.

'What?' I said, standing also.

'Mr Gold,' Suki was looking at me with wide eyes, 'it's . . .'

Fiona held up a hand to cut Suki off. And in that hand was a USB drive.

'What am I missing?' I said, totally not seeing whatever Suki had seen.

Fiona was grinning now, an uncomfortable grin, as though she was about to deliver the final nail in some poor soul's coffin, which I guess she probably was.

'My perverted sister,' she began, 'and her icky little dipping parties.'

The thought made me shudder.

'The first time, when she'd had the idea to be used and abused by strangers in such a way, she asked for it to be filmed, do you recall?'

I did. Suki had taken care of the whole thing. I'd seen the film; she'd done a good job of it. 'Yes,' I said.

'And she requested the strangers from Jessica Jones, yes?'

'That is correct.'

She handed me the USB. 'On the big screen, please.'

I took it from her. 'This is the film?'

'Not the original. I borrowed it from my sister's secret safe, and made a copy while she was at church discussing the wedding with the vicar.'

'Nice,' I said.

'The big screen,' she repeated.

I went to the monitor on the wall, plugged the USB into its side, and the video started playing.

There she was, Roz Winters, on her back on a low gurney, trussed up like a chicken, full leather head mask, pussy in the air. The camera followed the hands and the dicks of the men around her as they dipped and probed and licked at her mayo-filled pussy. Dipped carrot sticks. Dipped celery sticks. Dipped their grubby fingers and dicks into her before sucking each other off.

Fiona walked up to the screen, hovered a finger over the Pause button on the control panel. 'Any second now,' she said, and a flabby dick came into view, a guy with a paunch sinking his dick into her. And the camera panned back, just enough to capture the guy's face.

Fiona pressed Pause.

And that's when I saw it. Saw him. William Ripley dipping his wick into client number two.

'Holy shit indeed,' I said, repeating Suki's words. 'That's fucking shocking.'

Fiona pulled the USB. 'She can't marry that bastard,' she said. 'We can't let her.'

'We?'

'Yes, *we*.'

Suki suggested she should make us all some tea, and I agreed, needing time to get my head around the latest revelations.

'Why me?' I asked as we sat around my desk. 'You're her aunt, couldn't you take Emma to one side and–'

'And what? Come hither, oh favourite niece of mine, but just to let you know that your fiancé bums your daddy, oh, and he likes to fill your sweet mother's pussy with mayo and dip his sorry little wick until she pleads for more. As if that would do any good, Jonathon. Emma needs someone strong in her life, someone honest and good. She needs a life she can live, not an imposed prison, controlled by depraved money-hungry perverts.'

'But she'd listen to you,' I said.

'You don't get it, do you? If I told that little lot to Emma, her head would explode. She would go into denial. She would deny me. She would end up hating me and going ahead with the wedding anyway.'

'You don't seem to have much faith in her.'

'I know what her parents are like. Despicable people. Did you know that her father once threatened to shoot all of her horses unless she attended a private dinner where she would look her best and flutter her eyelashes at a prospective Saudi investor?'

'Shoot her horses?'

'And he would have. Emma doesn't know this, but he shot the family dog when she was little. All because it developed cataracts and could no longer join him on the hunt. Instead of retiring it to a life of warmth by the fireside, he took the dog out and shot it. Told Emma it had died in its sleep.'

'Maybe I should just shoot the bastard,' I said, and half meant it.

'We must tell Miss Emma everything,' Suki said.

'If only it was that simple,' I said.

'But why not?' she protested, the innocence in her eyes making me smile. 'The whole world should know.'

'What?' I said, 'Leak it to the press?'

Suki nodded. 'Anonymous. Then Miss Emma will find out.'

Fiona was shaking her head, 'That would never work, Suki.'

'Fiona's right,' I said, 'if we were to cause trouble for Emma's parents, or Ripley, if we were to expose them like that, they'd come down on us – on me – like a ton of bricks. We'd end up being shut down in one way or another, and a man capable of shooting the family dog, wouldn't take much goading to use that gun again.'

'Oh,' Suki said, 'this not fair situation.'

'Life's rarely fair,' Fiona said, 'but we have to do something, because Suki's right – the whole world *should* know, never mind just poor Emma. I want her out of that place, away from those people. I want her to have a good life.'

'And you thought I was the one to give her that?'

'No, Jonathon. I *know* you can give her that. And I know that she wants you. And I know that you want her.'

I couldn't deny it.

'The whole world should know,' Suki repeated.

And then it struck me. A bolt from the blue.

Call it a moment of madness, but there was a way to do this.

A brave way.

Foolish maybe.

The stuff of movies, maybe.

But there was a way to sweep Emma Jane off her feet and without any repercussions.

'You genius!' I said, 'Both of you.'

It was a crazy idea and sounded even crazier when I voiced it to Fiona and Suki.

Fiona clasped her mouth, then her heart, then she stomped around my office shouting 'Yes, yes, yes!' and she gave me a hug. 'Yes, let's do this.'

Suki's reaction wasn't dissimilar. 'Wow,' she'd said, 'holy fucking shit, Mr Gold,' she'd said.

Chapter Seventeen

Finding Nemo

Emma

My dress is truly beautiful – Italian satin in the palest cream, the slip dress embroidered with sequins the colours of Autumn, and the bodice a sheer overlay with Autumnal beading – it must have cost Aunt Fee an arm and a leg, but I felt like a sack of worthless shit. I could barely believe that I was going ahead with this.

'If you could link into your father and smile please.' The official photographer's eyes had never left my cleavage since we got here. A friend of William's apparently. I linked into my father, forced a smile and the camera's shutter clicked off numerous shots.

I'd busied myself with my horses this past week, stayed away from William as much as I could. Sometimes I found myself riding Gem out further than I ever had before. It was tempting to not go back.

But this was it. My big day. And I just wanted it over with.

'Hold your chin up a little . . . that's it, right there.' More camera flashes. And more still from the paps lining the wall of the church grounds. There was even a BBC News crew, for God's sake.

'And if I could have one last one with the veil down please, Miss Winters.'

I was glad to oblige. I dropped my veil and my smile along with it, and linked into Daddy while shutters whirred and the flashes went on forever.

The door to the church opened and Cameron stepped out, William's Best Man, a smarmy, public school toff with greased back hair and a pockmarked face. His eyes went straight to my tits. 'We're all ready for you inside,' he said, 'can we start the music?'

My legs were shaking, my heart pounding. I hadn't eaten for two days and was thankful, because I think I would have puked on Cameron's shiny shoes.

'Ready,' my father said, without even glancing at me. I gripped his arm tight, and thought of my horses.

Jonathon

'Are you okay?' Suki looked worried.

I took a drink of water, wiped the sweat from my brow. 'No.'

'No?'

'No. I'm fucking shitting myself.'

'You'll be fine.'

'Easy for you to say.'

'I'll be right there with you, Mr Gold. Nothing can go wrong.'

'Famous last words.'

'They'll be going in soon.' She turned the engine on.

We'd been here for over an hour, parked up away from the church, hidden behind the war memorial and an oak tree. I looked through the binoculars. Some ponce in a suit was talking to Emma and her father. The photographer slipped behind him and into the church. It was time. Shit.

I glanced at the piece of paper in my hands and tried to read through it one last time. My hands were trembling, my heart knocking so loud, I had to take some steadying breaths, and the words on the paper mixed themselves up and turned into something foreign.

'They're going in.' Suki pulled the jeep from its hiding place and drove us steadily down the narrow road to the church. As planned, she parked in a spot just yards from the gate, and pointed the jeep's nose in the direction of home.

'Ready?' she asked, holding out the DVD case.

'I don't know,' I said, glancing again at the piece of paper in my hands.

'Put it in your pocket,' Suki said, 'you've recited it a thousand times, you *will* be okay.'

I shoved it in my breast pocket, and took the DVD case from her.

'Mr Gold,' she put a hand on my arm. 'You going to be a hero!' And she smiled her ear to ear smile.

Emma

A sea of hats turned towards us. Gasps and murmurs of *doesn't she look beautiful*. And smiles. A church packed with gleaming smiles.

William waited for me, him and Cameron, their backs to me, facing Father Michael. William glanced over his shoulder, his smile more lecherous than loving. He turned back to the front, and in my mind I whipped a shotgun from under my dress and blasted a hole through his middle. Amidst the screams I calmly walked away. Gem was waiting for me at the door. Waiting to ride off into the sunset. Oh how I wished. But before I knew it we were there. Father letting go of me. No words. No kiss. And then I was by William's side. Cameron placing the rings on a cushion. And the music stopped.

Jonathon.

We slipped inside behind a few paps, and took up our positions in the back row. I guessed my face would be well-known by this time tomorrow.

I might have questioned my sanity at this point, but when the organ music stopped and Emma turned to face the despicable creep whose world I was about to threaten, my heart melted at her beauty. She looked stunning. And I . . . I loved her. I did. I truly loved her.

'Love,' the priest said, a voice so loud from such a diminutive man. 'Love,' he said again and all eyes were on him, 'is why we are here today.'

I wondered what Emma was thinking right now. Then doubt hit me like a kick in the nuts. What if she rejects me? What if she says *No*? What if I'm dragged away by her family as she laughs in my face? Am I doing the right thing? Jonathon Gold, you're fucking crazy. I glanced across the aisle to Suki. She was watching me through her sunglasses. She gave a solemn nod. Shit.

'In marriage, we not only say, *I love you today*, but, *I love you for all of our tomorrows*.'

I took the piece of paper from my pocket, focused on the words there, while the priest continued in a hazy background. I would keep the paper in my hand. That's what I'd do. Glance at it, if need be.

'William Ruben Ripley and Emma Jane Winters, I remind you that marriage is a precious gift . . .'

And above all, whatever you do, don't stall, Fiona had said. *When the priest utters those immortal words, you will not have time to dally*.

Yes. I knew that. The countdown had begun. Any minute now and I'd be either a hero or a fool. Jesus Christ Almighty, Jonathon. You better make this count.

'If anyone can show just cause why this couple cannot lawfully be joined together in matrimony . . .'

I took a breath, wet my lips, swallowed away the lump in my throat. The point of no return.

'. . . let him speak now or forever hold his peace.'

Emma

The silence was deathly. My breaths loud. I found myself wishing for a saviour. For the cops to rush in and arrest William for a heinous crime. For the church roof to fall in. For a zombie apocalypse. Anything. I looked to Father Michael, expecting him to continue. But he was staring down the aisle, brows furrowed. I followed his gaze to see the congregation turning their heads as one. Someone at the back had stood up.

'*Jon...*' his name left my lips in a whisper.

A vision in a light cream suit, a pale blue shirt, his dark hair ruffled. An angel walking down the aisle.

My legs were shaking. I grabbed Father Michael's arm.

Then the voices.

'What the hell?' Mother's exasperated hiss.

'Remove that man!' Father's boom echoed into the rafters.

'Shit,' William's only word.

'Stop him!' my father again.

But nobody stopped him. Camera flashes were going off at the back of the church. And the paps were following him down the aisle, cameras flashing like a trail of ethereal lights.

In the front row, Mother stood up and made to move, but Aunt Fee jumped to her feet and put an arm out to stop her. Mother blanched. I thought she might faint.

Father grunted out some choice words and made a move but Jonathon held up a hand. And in that hand was what looked like a DVD case, its cover white and blank. Father stopped dead. William was breathing heavy, his eyes scared and sharp.

I caught Aunt Fee's eye and she winked, and in that moment I felt a lightness in me. Felt lifted, like a bird about to be set free.

The congregation were chattering, mobile phones being held up, and despite my rocking heart, I found myself smiling.

'Quiet please,' Father Michael said loudly, and the chatter ceased.

'I will not tolerate–' my father started but Father Michael cut him off with a raised hand.

'Let me repeat,' he said to the room, 'if anyone can show just cause why this couple cannot lawfully be joined together in matrimony . . . let him speak now or forever hold his peace.'

'I have something to say,' Jonathon said. His dark eyes were on mine, nervous yet firm, intense. So intense I wanted to run to him.

He slipped the DVD into his pocket.

'This is preposterous,' Father said.

'Mr Winters,' Father Michael said. 'Let this man have his say or I will ask you to leave.'

Father glanced at Mother. Mother looked scared, really scared. And I was glad.

'Please continue,' Father Michael said.

Jon gave an appreciative nod. He wet his lips and looked at my father. 'To Mr Winters, I want to ask a favour. And I know that I'm asking someone who likes to ask favours himself. So I know you will appreciate where I'm coming from when I ask, sir, that you do me a favour and allow your daughter to make her own choices from this moment on.'

My father had blanched as well, a mixture of fear and fury on his face. I was glad of that, too.

'To Mr Ripley,' Jon's eyes were now on William, and William looked petrified. And I was still smiling. 'Mr Ripley, I respectfully suggest,' Jon paused for a breath – or for effect – as his voice carried through the church and his audience waited with bated breath, 'that when looking for a mate, one's culinary tastes should be considered.'

William's face had frozen. Aunt Fee looked delighted.

'You strike me,' Jon went on, 'as more a mayo dip kind of guy.'

A small gasp from Mother. She sat back down and shrank into her chair.

'Whereas Emma Jane here, she likes, well . . .' Jon looked at me, a twitch of a smile, 'Emma has more taste.'

I didn't have a clue what he was taking about, but Father, Mother, and William were silenced and scared, I could smell their fear.

'Is this relevant at all?' Father Michael said, and I almost hushed him myself.

'Very,' Jon said.

'I'm sorry, young man, but you're talking in riddles. If you know of any unlawful–'

'There's been a mistake,' Jon said. 'In fact, there's been a few. And I'm here to put that right. So please, hear me out.'

Father Michael nodded, and I clasped my small bouquet to my chest, eyes pricking with tears. I didn't know what was going on, but I felt every moment, felt Jonathon, wanted him.

He took another two steps forward, only feet away from me now.

'You have good friends,' he said, smiling at me. At the back of the room a small figure stepped into the aisle. A summery dress, sunglasses, and a headscarf. Suki. My heart leapt. She held a hand out to her side, the keys to her jeep swinging from a finger. 'Good friends forever.'

'Yes,' I whispered.

'You have a choice,' Jon said, 'and I assure you, that if you make the choice that I and your good friends hope you make, you will be safe. Completely safe.'

'Safe,' I heard myself say.

'I'm sure, that no one here will object to my asking,' he glanced at William, at Father, at Mother. 'Emma Jane, I . . . I want . . . I ask with all my heart . . . that you marry me. I love you, and I want you to be my wife.'

A chorus of gasps. Someone cheered. Father Michael's hands were tight around my arm. I realised he was holding me up.

But no one was objecting. Not William. Not Father. Not Mother. And Aunt Fee's hands were at her mouth, her grin deliriously wide.

'Emma?'

'Your wife?' I said, my trembling voice not my own.

'I love you,' he said again.

My bouquet fell, bounced away from me.

I lifted my dress and kicked my heels off and ran to him.

Fell into strong arms. Laughed as he picked me up and twirled me round.

And then we were running, following Suki through the doorway, camera flashes following us, and the church resounded with cheers and applause as we dashed into the sunlight and ran hand in hand down the path and through the gates and into Suki's jeep, the back door waiting open, Suki at the wheel, revving the engine as we dived inside.

Suki drove off at speed and I grabbed Jon and hugged him and kissed him but he stopped me.

'Just a second,' he said and pulled the DVD case from his pocket. He looked out the back window. At least three cars were following. And more paps were getting in their cars and pulling into the road.

Jon wound his window down and held the DVD case out so our pursuers would see it, then he flung it out, spinning through the air to land on the grass verge.

The first car stopped and so did those behind and there was a mad scramble of paps as we disappeared around the corner.

'What was on the DVD?' I asked.

'Finding Nemo,' Jon said, 'bought it at the petrol station this morning, turned the cover inside out.'

'Whoopeeeeee!' Suki yelled, and I laughed, And Jon laughed. And we laughed all the way home.

Home.

THE END

Epilogue

Emma

The old stables around the back hadn't been used in decades, but with thirty angels mucking in they were soon mucked out, repaired, cleaned and painted, the yard scrubbed and the horses moved in.

Suki and Jonathon were both engrossed in learning to ride, and Suki was my permanent PA. Life was rosy. Oh, and Aunt Fee found a new cock in Angel Harry, who turned out to be Suki's cousin. We do like to keep it in the family.

Jonathon had told me everything, shocking as it was. The strange thing was, my father's shares and those of Ripley's Gum & Candy went through the roof after the tabloids spoke of *true love*, and *an angel in white*. Front page. Jonathon twirling me around, a camera flash like a halo above his head. We had that enlarged and framed on the office wall. *Our* office wall. And we never heard a peep from from my parents or from William Ripley.

'Are you sure about this?' Jon asked, looking down at his naked self. Naked apart from his riding boots.

'You look beautiful,' I said and went to him. Our boots touched, as did our nakedness. I wrapped my arms around his neck and kissed him, his tongue searching, his arousal instant, nudging at my tummy.

'You're crazy,' he said.

'Crazy for you.'

I reached below and took him in my hand, worked him hard and kissed him some more. 'Ready?'

He smiled that lovely dimpled smile. 'As I'll ever be.'

I led him from the stable to the awaiting Gem. She snorted her approval as I patted her neck and then mounted her. Jonathon followed, settled into position behind me and I slid easily onto him.

'That feels good,' he said.

'Always,' I agreed, and clenched at him.

He groaned and pressed his lips to my back, sending shivers to my tits. 'Not too fast, ay?' he said, taking hold of my hips.

'Yeah, nice and easy,' I said and nudged Gem into a walk.

The night was warm, the air still, the sun an orange glow on the horizon.

We left the yard and Gem picked it up a little when her hooves felt the grass. I reined her back, kept her steady.

'You ready?'

Jonathon gripped my waist, pushed himself into me. 'This is one way to ride off into the sunset.'

I wriggled on his cock, lifted his hands from my waist to my tits, and tapped Gem into a canter.

He squeezed at my tits. 'I fucking love you,' he said with a grunt as I bucked onto him.

'I fucking love you too, Mr Gold.'

Acknowledgements

I must thank the force behind the birth and nurturing of *Six*, without whom Six would either be decidedly lame or non-existent. So, to my initial brilliant betas: Jade, Siobhan, and Tracy, who whipped my ass relentlessly, who tutted and groaned at all the right places until I had no choice but to perform, I thank you profusely.

To my dogged street team, the Juicy Ladies that are Michelle and Lesley, thank you for your tireless support. I appreciate *everything* that you do.

Thank you also to the Crowgirl betas for some amazing reviews and for spotting those typos. (Special mention to Sherlock McGinty for going the extra mile and ruining her fine-tooth comb in the process. If you ever lose a needle in a haystack, she's your gal.)

Huge thanks to Beth, for keeping me right and for doing all the other jobs so that I can keep on writing. Beth you are pure Gold!

And finally a very special thank you and eternal gratefulness to the inimitable Jade West for taking me by the hand and *teaching me dirty*. You did a reasonable job, I think.

Oh, and I can't forget Roz, the spark to my bark. *Good girl.*

About the Author

James Crow lives in the UK in a redbrick mansion, where the walls are tall, the basements deep, and where secrets aplenty are just waiting to be told. Watch this space.

18181403R00133

Printed in Great Britain
by Amazon